Maitlyn suddenly clutched the front of her shirt with both hands, as she shifted her weight from one leg to the other. "I shouldn't have come downstairs," she abruptly rambled, her voice barely a whisper. "I don't know what I was thinking. This isn't like me."

"No, it's not, but you're doing fine." Zak's tone was intense. He tried to catch her eye, but she looked away, her nerves beginning to get the best of her. He flashed a bright smile, but she still felt apprehensive. He stepped in closer to her, and Maitlyn dropped her arms against her sides and clenched her hands into a fist. They were clasped together so tightly that she could feel the blood pulsing through her fingertips.

She'd been committed when she'd come down the stairs, but her self-assurance was melting. She was like a blushing bride, virginal and timid. She'd descended the steps with a purpose, and now she seemed unwilling or simply unable to initiate the first touch.

So, he did.

Books by Deborah Fletcher Mello

Harlequin Kimani Arabesque

Forever and a Day
The Right Side of Love
A Love for All Time
Take Me to Heart

Harlequin Kimani Romance

In the Light of Love
Always Means Forever
To Love a Stallion
Tame a Wild Stallion
Lost in a Stallion's Arms
Promises to a Stallion
Seduced by a Stallion
Forever a Stallion
Passionate Premiere
Truly Yours
Hearts Afire

DEBORAH FLETCHER MELLO

Writing since forever, Deborah Fletcher Mello can't imagine herself doing anything else. Her first romance novel, *Take Me To Heart,* earned her a 2004 Romance Slam Jam nomination for Best New Author. In 2005 she received Book of the Year and Favorite Heroine nominations for her novel *The Right Side of Love,* and in 2009 won an RT Reviewers' Choice Award for her ninth novel, *Tame A Wild Stallion.* With fifteen romances under her belt, Deborah continues to create unique storylines and memorable characters.

For Deborah, writing is as necessary as breathing, and she firmly believes that if she could not write she would cease to exist. For Deborah, the ultimate thrill is to weave a story that leaves her audience feeling full, and satisfied, as if they've just enjoyed an incredible meal. Born and raised in Connecticut, Deborah now considers home to be wherever the moment moves her.

DEBORAH
FLETCHER
MELLO

HARLEQUIN® KIMANI™ ROMANCE

To my pretty, pretty princess,
JoAnna Alaina Woody
Your beautiful smile just warms MeeMi's heart!

Recycling programs
for this product may
not exist in your area.

ISBN-13: 978-0-373-86341-9

HEARTS AFIRE

Copyright © 2014 by Deborah Fletcher Mello

For questions and comments about the quality of this book please contact us at CustomerService@Harlequin.com.

HARLEQUIN®
www.Harlequin.com

Printed in U.S.A.

Dear Reader,

Thank you! I am so humbled by your continued support. Thank you for sharing my stories, and enabling my fan base to grow. Please know that your reviews, critiques and comments on social media sites have helped me get better with each new story.

I am *loving* the Boudreaux family. I love that I am able to breathe life into each of the siblings' unique personalities. I had thought I knew Maitlyn, but then both she and Zak Sayed took me by surprise. This couple came with some unique and conflicting personality traits. Staying true to that and making their story believable was not without challenges, but I hope you'll agree it was well worth the effort.

Until the next time, please take care and may God's many blessings continue to be with you.

With much love,

Deborah Fletcher Mello

DeborahMello@aol.com
www.DeborahMello.blogspot.com
www.Twitter.com/DebbMelloWrites
www.Facebook.com/DeborahFletcherMello

Chapter 1

Maitlyn let out a deep sigh, and her brow furrowed as she read through the legal documents that dissolved her marriage and gave her back her family name.

The day she'd married Donald Parks all Maitlyn had dreamed of was the two of them having two kids, a dog and the house with the white picket fence. And now, here she was, grateful that they had never had children together. She would not have wanted to subject any child to the catastrophe that had been their marriage. She sighed once more before lifting her dark eyes to meet her sister's intense gaze.

District court judge Katrina Stallion was eyeing her critically; her expression voiced her concerns even before she spoke. "You will keep your home here, your brownstone in Harlem and your Los Angeles properties. Donald will keep the town house in Atlanta. Any ties he had with the Maitlyn Agency have now been completely severed. You've agreed to reimburse the ten thousand he initially invested in your company, and he's agreed that he will have no claims on any future royalties or benefits from the business. But you are still legally entitled to half his pension and retirement benefits from his employment with IBM. The state considers it all community property and therefore subject to division. Once you give me the word, I'll draw up the paperwork and file for a court order adjunct to the divorce decree."

Maitlyn shook her head. "I don't want it. I don't want *anything* from Donald."

Their mother's voice interjected from across the room. Katherine Boudreaux stood in front of her kitchen sink, her forearms lost in a bath of soapy water as she washed the dishes left from breakfast. "Maitlyn, before you make a final decision you need to take some time to think about it. You were a good wife. Every tear that man made you cry earned you that money. There is no reason you shouldn't claim it."

Katherine turned to stare at her fourth child. "She doesn't have to make a decision right now, does she, Katrina?" she asked.

"No, ma'am. We can make note that we'll be filing for an amendment to the settlement agreement later. It's just important that Maitlyn knows what her rights are and what she's legally entitled to."

Katherine nodded as she reached for a dish towel to dry her hands. "Good, then she can decide when she comes back."

Both women turned to eye the older woman curiously.

"Back from where, Mom?" Katrina asked.

"Where am I going?" Maitlyn questioned.

Katherine smiled brightly as she tossed the dishrag back on the counter. "It's a surprise from your father. Let me go find Senior so he can tell you himself," she said as she disappeared out the back door of the kitchen.

Maitlyn rolled her eyes.

Katrina chuckled softly. "Those are *your* parents," she said teasingly.

Maitlyn smiled ever so slightly, feigning interest in the conversation as she pondered what their parents might have in store for her. Truth be told, Maitlyn didn't like surprises, and she really didn't care to discover what this one might be. She was still completely distraught over finding herself single and alone after twelve years of marriage to the only man she had ever loved.

When Maitlyn had made the decision to finally dissolve her marriage, Katrina, still legally able to practice law in the state of Louisiana, had flown in from her Dallas home to represent her. Providing a wealth of emotional support, Katrina had helped to ease the hurt that came when the life Maitlyn had once envisioned for herself had fallen completely apart. "What were you saying about John and Marah?" she asked as Katrina continued to update her on the latest family news.

Katrina was married to Matthew Stallion of the renowned Stallion family out of Texas. The couple had two children: seventeen-year old Collin from Katrina's first marriage and their new baby, Matthew Jacoby Junior, who would soon be celebrating his first birthday. Their oldest brother, Mason Boudreaux, was married to Matthew's younger sister, Phaedra, and the couple had already been planning the perfect time to conceive their first child. They had been watching the moon and stars and taking fertility advice from their sister Kamaya, and Maitlyn fathomed it would only be a matter of time before they'd be making their big announcement. Babies were suddenly becoming quite the rage between the two families. But Katrina had just mentioned something about the oldest brother, John Stallion, and his wife, Marah…something about them not being able to have any children.

Katrina released a loud sigh. "I swear, Maitlyn. I've been talking to you for ten minutes and you haven't paid attention to a word I've said!"

"Yes, I was," Maitlyn professed. "I just—I…" she stammered. She then swiped at a tear that had rolled down her cheek. "Donald didn't want kids, but he didn't bother to tell me that until after we were married. When it became an issue between us he went and had a vasectomy without even discussing it with me first."

"He didn't tell you?" Katrina gasped.

Maitlyn nodded. "Donald did a lot of things he didn't bother to tell me about."

Her sister shook her head. "Maitlyn, why didn't you tell any of us? We're your family, and if you had just opened up, you know we would have been there for you."

Maitlyn shrugged. "I know. I just…" She trailed off as she shrugged her shoulders. The words had caught in her chest as she struggled not to cry. She couldn't begin to explain how she felt. As the second child and the eldest girl, she was the one who was supposed to be there for her siblings to depend on. If they had been aware of her failings, how could they have trusted her to be there for them in their times of need?

Katrina tapped the documents on the table. "Well, that phase of your life is done and finished. Leave the past behind you. You need to live your dreams now!"

Maitlyn nodded as she forced a smile. She took a

deep breath and cleared her throat. "So, what were you saying about Marah?"

"Marah and John found out that they can't have kids. She has some kind of uterine abnormality that will make it difficult for her to carry a child to term."

Maitlyn suddenly struggled again to fight back her tears. "That's so sad," she said. "They seem so happy together, and the last time I talked to her she said they were really trying to have a baby."

"It is sad," Katrina agreed. "But they're handling it well. Marah was telling me that they've discussed adoption and surrogacy and are considering their options. But neither of them seemed overly concerned. And when you consider that John's already raised a family, you can better understand why it might not bother them as much. After all, John was seventeen and his youngest brother, Luke, was just six when their parents died. John stepped in to take full responsibility for his brothers."

"But what about Marah? How does she feel? It has to bother her, right?"

"Sometimes when she's babysitting Jake, I can see the sadness in her eyes. She says that between running the ranch and her business that she barely has time to take care of herself let alone a baby, but you never know. Right now, they're taking some alone time in Paris, so we'll see what happens when they get back."

"She's going to miss having kids," Maitlyn professed, her voice dropping to a low whisper. "I know I do."

Katrina tossed her a slight smile. "Having children is still an option for you. You deserve to be happy, Maitlyn. It's time you looked forward to what's ahead for you. You don't need to worry over your past anymore."

Maitlyn nodded her head. "I know."

"I'm going to tell you like I told Marah and like Mommy has always told all of us. Trust in whatever plan *God* has for you."

Before Maitlyn could respond, her father's booming voice resounded from the doorway. The two women turned to see Mason "Senior" Boudreaux making his way into the room. He cradled Katrina's young son in his arms. The baby was laughing heartily as drool flooded down his chin. Senior tickled his chubby folds, and the baby laughed again. The sight of them made both women laugh.

"Me and baby Jake were trying to stay away from all your girl stuff. Men can't get no kind of peace in this house!"

"Stop your fussing," Katherine admonished as she moved in behind them. She reached to wipe the baby's mouth with the corner of his bib.

Katrina cut an eye toward her big sister and smiled. "So, where is Mattie going, Senior? What's the big surprise?"

Senior met his daughter's curious gaze as Maitlyn stared at him past her sister's shoulder. "Should I be scared?" she questioned.

Senior laughed as he blew bubbles against the baby's cheek. "I would be. That's a whole lot of water you gone be on!"

"Water? I don't understand—" Maitlyn started.

Katherine clapped her hands together excitedly. "Senior is sending you on a cruise. You leave at the end of the week," she exclaimed.

Katrina jumped up with excitement. Completely

stunned, Maitlyn came to her feet, as well. "A cruise? I can't do a cruise," she stated.

Senior passed baby Jake to Katrina. He took a deep breath as he moved to stand in front of his oldest daughter; then his hands gripped her gently by the shoulders. "You *can* do a cruise, and you *will* do this cruise."

"But, Senior, I have to work! I can't just—"

The patriarch held up his index finger and shook it in her face. "You need some time away, Maitlyn Rose. You've had a rough year. Your mama and I have been watching you take care of everyone but yourself. Between managing Guy's career, cleaning up Darryl's messes, handling Kamaya's business and everything else you do for your brothers and sisters, not to mention your other clients, you haven't had any time for you. And that stops right now."

"Your father's right," Katherine interjected. "With everything Donald put you through, this will be a great opportunity for Maitlyn to rediscover Maitlyn. You need to do you a Stella!"

Katrina suddenly laughed out loud, her eyes wide with amusement.

Maitlyn looked confused. "Stella? What does that mean?"

Katherine rolled her eyes. "Go get your groove back, baby."

Color flushed Maitlyn's face as understanding washed over her.

Senior reached for his grandson again and moved back toward the door. "Come on, Jake. Told you we men can't get a minute of peace with all these women in the house," he chimed as they disappeared from view.

Katrina laughed again. "Mama, I think you embarrassed Senior."

Maitlyn nodded as she sat back down. "I know you embarrassed me!"

Katherine fanned a hand at her daughters. "You know your daddy better than that." She dropped down onto the seat beside Maitlyn and wrapped an arm around her shoulders.

"And I don't know what you're embarrassed about. That well has been dry for too long," she teased. "It's time you go get yours, baby. That's all I'm going to say." Katherine leaned in to kiss her daughter's cheek. "Go get yours!"

Shaking her head, Maitlyn smiled ever so slightly as Katherine and Katrina both laughed out loud.

Standing in front of the full-length mirror that hung from the closet door, Maitlyn held up two dresses, flashing one and then the other in front of her lean frame.

"Pack them both," Tarah Boudreaux said. "In fact, pack it all! You'll be gone for thirty-four days. For thirty-four days you're going to need a lot of clothes. No one expects you to pack conservatively."

"No one expects me to go over my baggage limit, either. I don't know why I agreed to do this," Maitlyn exclaimed, dropping down onto the full-size bed. "I don't want to do this!"

Tarah laughed. "Do you want to tell Senior that, or do you want me to tell him for you?"

"Would it make a difference?"

"Nope. He'll still tell you that you're going whether you like it or not." Tarah giggled.

Maitlyn sighed as she threw herself back against the

mattress. She pulled an arm across her face, covering her eyes. She wanted to be excited about her trip, but she was still mourning the loss of her marriage. Life had thrown her a serious curve, and she wasn't quite ready to end the pity party she'd been throwing for herself.

Her ex-husband's rejection had been monumental, and she was tired of pretending to be strong when all she felt was broken. She took a deep breath as she sat upright and met the harsh stare Tarah was giving her. Like the rest of her family, Tarah refused to commiserate, totally unconcerned with her discontent. "What?" she questioned, eyeing her sister with annoyance.

"I think we should go lingerie shopping. You can't pack any of this stuff," her baby sister said, shaking a fistful of her cotton panties in the air.

Maitlyn rolled her eyes. "Why are you touching my underwear?"

"Because these granny panties are not cute! And you definitely don't want to be caught wearing these if you should meet a guy on your cruise."

Maitlyn shook her head, not at all amused.

"Oh, oh, oh," Tarah suddenly exclaimed, jumping onto the bed beside her. "I think you should have sex with one of the cabin guys."

"I am not having sex with a cabin guy."

"Just wild, dirty sex where you don't even bother to ask his name," Tarah said excitedly, her hands waving in the air. "I can just see it now. He won't know you're in the room when he comes into your cabin to turn down the bed. You'll pretend to be surprised when he catches you doing this sultry striptease out of your clothes. Then you'll give him a sexy *come-hither* look, and when he does you rip his uniform off. Afterward, you show him to the door and leave him a big tip so he definitely knows it wasn't a love thing."

"Do you hear yourself?' Maitlyn asked with her eyebrows lifted in astonishment.

"The more important question is do *you* hear me?"

"Reel in that creative imagination of yours, please. This is not what this trip is for, Tarah. I swear, Mommy and Daddy taught you better."

Tarah laughed. "Exactly! How often do Mommy and Daddy give you carte blanche approval to go do your thing with no repercussions? You can go have sex with the cabin boy, the pool guy *and* the captain and no one will say anything because they won't know unless you tell! What happens on the cruise stays on the cruise. Isn't that what Mommy said?"

"You are so silly," Maitlyn said, her smile wide.

"Just wild, dirty sex with no strings. Oh, yeah! Go, Maitlyn! Go, Maitlyn!" Tarah sang. "Get your groove on!"

Tarah's gleeful tone made Maitlyn laugh out loud. "Anyway, how's school?" she asked, hoping to divert her sister's attention to something else.

"School is fine. Don't change the subject."

Maitlyn tossed up her hands. "I'm not talking about this anymore, Tarah."

"Don't talk, just keep packing, and then let's go shopping. I feel a Victoria's Secret shopping spree coming on," Tarah said as she scrambled off the bed and headed toward the door. "I'll go see if Mommy and Katrina want to come." Tarah raced out the door.

Maitlyn smiled. Despite her best efforts it looked like her self-proclaimed pity party was about to come to an end.

Chapter 2

Even with the enthusiasm her family had been projecting over her impending trip, Maitlyn was more convinced than ever that the month-long excursion was not a good idea. As she approached the docks, she couldn't begin to fathom what she would do with herself for all that time. She was half tempted to say so out loud when Tarah interrupted her thoughts with a squeal of excitement.

"There's your ship! Look how big it is!" Tarah chimed, pointing out the window of their brother's SUV.

Peering where her sister pointed, Maitlyn was suddenly overwhelmed with emotion; the sheer size of the luxury cruise liner took her breath away. The *Coastal Galaxy,* ranked as one of the world's largest vessels, towered above the shoreline. The megaship looked like a floating skyscraper lying sideways.

Kendrick Boudreaux laughed as he navigated his car into the Port of New Orleans and headed toward the Julia Street cruise terminal. He pulled into a no-parking zone, shut down the engine and jumped swiftly out of the vehicle.

Maitlyn tossed her sister a look and shook her head. "Only *your* brother," she said matter-of-factly.

They both watched as Kendrick shook hands with the traffic officer on duty. The two men exchanged words before he returned and opened the rear hatch to the automobile.

"You're going to get a ticket," Maitlyn said.

Kendrick laughed. "No, I'm not," he responded casually.

"How are you *not* going to get a ticket?" Tarah questioned, cutting an eye toward Maitlyn.

Their brother smiled and winked and then passed Maitlyn's luggage to a porter, who seemed almost too eager to be of assistance. Kendrick was the master of not answering questions. Tarah was used to it, but it galled Maitlyn to no end. Her eyes narrowed in annoyance as she dug into her handbag for a tip, but the man and her luggage were gone before she could get her hand out of her billfold.

Kendrick laughed. "What's wrong, Mattie? You're usually on top of your game. You seem a little slow this morning."

"I don't know what I'm doing," she admitted. "And I definitely don't know why I agreed to do this!"

Her brother shook his head, dropping his large hands against the curve of her shoulders. "Go have yourself a good time."

"How can I have a good time when I don't even know what it is I'm supposed to be doing every day?"

Tarah jumped up excitedly. "We took care of that," she said as she passed her sister the bag with all her travel documents. "Me, Mom and Katrina have booked you for all the spa treatments and offshore excursions. You're going to have a blast!"

"All of them?"

"Well, the good ones," Tarah responded, shrugging her shoulders easily.

Kendrick laughed, shaking her lightly before wrapping his arms around her in a warm hug. "It's going to be okay. Just go have fun!"

In that moment Maitlyn couldn't fathom what *fun* might entail. But she had to admit that all her sister's teasing had her fantasizing about a prospective encounter that might leave her completely satisfied without the burdens of commitment. Wild, passionate sex with a nameless, hard body just might be the kind of medicine she needed to get past the drama that had been her life. And if she could have wild, passionate sex with a stranger and never have anyone in her family find out, then why not, she reasoned. Her thoughts were interrupted when Kendrick suddenly did an about-face and called out to a stranger who was handing off his own luggage to a porter.

"Zakaria?"

"Kendrick Boudreaux!"

Kendrick moved forward in greeting and eagerly shook the handsome stranger's hand. The two slapped palms and gave each other a warm hug.

Maitlyn took a step forward, staring at where the two stood. Both men had clearly captured the attention of everyone around them. Her brother's good looks had never fazed her, but his friend, with his warm complexion, luxurious black curly hair and his chiseled features, was tall, dark and handsome to the nth degree. Behind her, Tarah murmured under her breath, "My, my, my!"

Both women stood back as the two men fell into conversation. Maitlyn cut her eye toward Tarah, who was grinning like the Cheshire cat as she moved her body in closer and leaned heavily against her arm and shoulder. Mischief danced in the younger woman's dark eyes.

"Don't you dare," Maitlyn admonished between clenched teeth.

Tarah giggled, whispering back, "I was just going to say that you might want to rethink doing it with the cabin guy and consider doing it with *that* guy."

Kendrick suddenly gestured in their direction.

"Maitlyn, let me introduce you. This is Zakaria Sayed. Zak and I did some business together years ago, and we've been friends ever since. Zak, this is my sister Maitlyn Boudreaux. This is her first cruise."

"It's a pleasure to meet you, Ms. Boudreaux," Zak said as he wrapped a large palm around her hand, his dark gaze meeting hers evenly.

"It's very nice to meet you, too," Maitlyn murmured, heat wafting in a large wave up her spine. She pulled her hand from his, her fingers tingling from his touch. She clenched her fist, drawing her hand behind her back to stall the sensation. Her eyes were still locked with his.

Tarah cleared her throat, her eyebrows lifted.

Kendrick laughed. "Oh, and that's Tarah, our baby sister."

"Hey," Tarah exclaimed, waving her hand in greeting as the man turned his attention in her direction. "So will you be cruising today, too, Mr. Sayed?"

"Please, call me Zak," he said. His tone was deep and rich, a melodic vibrato that would have been perfect for a late-night radio program. "And, yes, I'll be traveling on this cruise."

Kendrick interjected, "Zak is participating in the World Series of Poker tournament. He's made it to the grand finale, which will be played out on the ship."

"You're a professional gambler?" Maitlyn questioned, curiosity peaking her interest.

The man's smile was brilliant as he tilted his head to stare down at her. His deep gaze caused her breath to halt and air to catch in her chest.

"I would not call myself a professional," he said, the deep timbre of his voice heating her feminine spirit. "I'm just a man who likes a challenge," he professed.

Maitlyn felt herself nodding, her head moving up and down foolishly. She was grateful when her brother interjected.

"Mattie, Zak has promised to keep an eye on you, so I know you'll be in good hands."

Her eyes widened as she forced herself to smile. "That's very kind, Mr. Sayed, but my little brother shouldn't have imposed on you. I really don't need a babysitter." She cut an eye at Kendrick, whose mocking gaze made her want to give him a good punch.

Zak chuckled softly. "That's a good thing, Ms. Boudreaux. I had no plans to babysit anyone on this trip," he said matter-of-factly.

Kendrick laughed. "Well, you two had better head inside," he said, glancing down to the gold watch on his wrist. He leaned in to kiss her cheek. "Have a great trip," he chimed.

Maitlyn hugged him and then Tarah.

Her sister moved in to whisper into her ear. "Tap that," she murmured under her breath. *"Pleeeease!"*

Taking a deep breath, Maitlyn could only shake her head. She tossed one last look over her shoulder at her brother and sister, who were waving excitedly as she proceeded to board the ship.

She was suddenly aware of the warm palm Zak Sayed had rested against her elbow as he led her through the doors into the terminal. Neither spoke a word as they cleared the metal detectors and checked in at the registration desk. Maitlyn was surprised when he paused to wait for her after they were pointed in the direction of the gangway, especially since he had yet to utter one word to her. His expression was nondescript; the man seemed focused on something other than her.

But Maitlyn couldn't comment, either. She found herself completely tongue-tied in his presence. She took a deep breath and held it, fighting the wave of anxiety that threatened to consume her.

Suddenly a wide-eyed redhead rushed over, greeting them cheerily. "Hello! Welcome to Coastal Cruise Lines," the chipper attendant chimed.

"Thank you," Zak responded politely.

"Let's get your arrival photo taken care of and then you can board," the young woman said as her associate guided them both in front of a cardboard stand-up of the cruise line's logo.

"Just stand a little closer to your husband," the other woman said as she pushed them side by side.

"Oh, he's not… We're not…" Maitlyn stammered. Her widened eyes made her look like a deer caught in headlights. She tossed a quick glance up at Zak, who was smiling. Maitlyn found herself completely smitten by the sheer beauty of it.

Zak winked his eye at her as he slipped an arm around her waist and pulled her closer. If he hadn't been holding on to her, Maitlyn swore she would have dropped straight to the floor, as her knees quivered like two rubber bands.

Minutes later the two stepped onto the ship, and the cruise director greeted Zak by name.

"Mr. Sayed, welcome aboard, sir," the woman said. "My name's Stacy."

Zak nodded.

Stacy then gestured to the man at her side. "David will take you to your cabin, sir. If you follow him down the stairwell to the lower lobby, you'll take those elevators to the seventeenth floor and your suite, which is on the aft end of the ship. And if there is anything we can get for you, please don't hesitate to ask."

"Thank you," Zak answered. He then turned his attention toward Maitlyn. "I look forward to seeing you again, Ms. Boudreaux. Enjoy your cruise," he said casually.

Maitlyn smiled politely as he turned and left her and the cruise director standing together. The woman glanced politely at Maitlyn's boarding pass and pointed her in the opposite direction. Maitlyn shook her head, disappointment painting her expression. Sure, she hadn't expected the man to walk her to the door of her cabin, but she also hadn't anticipated him dismissing her so casually. The fact that she was even disturbed by his actions at all unnerved her because clearly Zak Sayed was a man who was more trouble than he was worth.

As Stacy moved to help another vacationer, Maitlyn moved to stand in front of the bank of elevator doors.

Behind the closed door of his luxury suite, Zak took quick note of the two-deck-high stateroom with its panoramic views. The lower-level living space with the private balcony, dining area and bar would be ideal for entertaining if he felt inclined to do that kind of thing. The upper level boasted a king-size bed and shower large enough for two people to lose themselves in. The space would serve him nicely on the trip, he thought. He slid open the glass door to the balcony and stepped out to peer over the edge of the rail. The water below sloshed lazily against the side of the massive cruise ship.

Hours earlier his thoughts had only been on the high-stakes poker game he was taking part in and the ten million dollars that had secured his participation. But since exiting the limo that delivered him to the docks, he'd thought less about the poker game and more about the beautiful woman who'd boarded the ship with him. A smile lifted his lips.

He and Kendrick Boudreaux shared much history. Kendrick's business dealings had brought him to Zak's family home in Morocco. At that time he had been brokering an arms deal between two political entities. Their initial encounter might not have gone well had Kendrick not been so open and forthcoming. Zak had learned much about the man during that time, and the family he spoke of so highly. Zak also remembered how fondly he had spoken about his sisters, yet he didn't remember Kendrick ever mentioning them being so beautiful.

Thoughts of the lovely Maitlyn Boudreaux passed through his mind. He had turned to stare after her just before heading to his cabin and had been taken aback by the overwhelming sadness he saw on her face. He couldn't begin to imagine what had soured her spirit, but he didn't want to see that look on her face ever again.

He also found it curious that she was traveling alone.

Most of the beautiful women he knew would have been hard-pressed to travel all by their lonesome with no kind of entourage by their side. Most especially for the length of time they would be at sea. Zak fathomed that a woman with such confidence could either be quite intriguing or an annoyance for a man. It was a rare male who could handle a woman with such bold conviction, or who even wanted to. His lips bent slightly upward at the thought.

But concerning himself with any woman was not something he had time for. This trip wasn't about a good time. Zak was on a mission, and until the last card was dealt and the final hand played, that was all he could afford to concentrate on. He had far too much money on the line to allow the prospect of a woman to distract him. Shaking thoughts of Maitlyn Boudreaux from his mind, he moved back inside his cabin and secured the sliding glass doors.

After managing to find her cabin before the ship left the dock, Maitlyn was greeted at the door by Winston, the cabin steward, who wasn't at all bad on the eyes. The young man's spirited personality even had her briefly contemplating her sister's suggestions. Because for the first time in a very long time, Maitlyn was willing to admit that she had needs that could use some serious attention. And she had Zak Sayed's touch to thank for the reminder.

Left on her own, Maitlyn quickly deposited her carry-on in her room and went to explore her surroundings. As she toured, she became completely enamored by the sheer size of the massive cruise ship and all the attention the cruise staff lavished on her. She thought about what it might feel like to have a man, perhaps one like Zak Sayed, to experience the moment with.

She sighed deeply as she took a quick glance around her, hoping that no one had been watching as decadent thoughts had washed over her spirit. She imagined herself naked, enjoying the pleasure of a hard-bodied male alongside her. Her cheeks flushed a deep red. Maitlyn was suddenly embarrassed that she'd even allowed herself to give such nonsense any consideration. And then she wasn't, pondering how she might make such an encounter occur.

Leaning against the rail that bordered the upper deck, she stared out to where the skyline kissed the sea and the sun began its descent in the bright blue sky. Closing her eyes briefly, she took a deep breath and then a second. She prayed that taking this trip would be a good thing for her. Her parents had never steered her wrong before, and she couldn't fathom them doing so now.

As she stared back out over the water, the moment was interrupted when a uniformed waiter suddenly appeared at her elbow, a pretty drink decorated with a paper parasol in hand. He pointed in the direction of the man who had sent the beverage. The gentleman nodded his head as he gestured toward the empty seat at his side. His inviting smile was miles wide. With his linebacker's build, blond hair and eyes that were as blue as the ocean water, he made quite a first impression. Nodding her gratitude, Maitlyn lifted her mouth in an appreciative smile. She then tossed her reservations aside and moved in the man's direction.

Chapter 3

Something in the glass she was holding was guiding Maitlyn's hips in a sexy shimmy that had the full attention of every man in the room. The reggae band performing on the stage had her mesmerized as she commanded the dance floor, her sensual moves in sync with the beat.

Zak had taken notice of her the moment he'd walked into the ship's nightclub. He had sat alone, and the ice in his drink was beginning to melt. A few days had passed since he'd last seen her and as he watched her from a table in the far corner of the room he thought back to earlier in the week when they'd first arrived together.

She was still strikingly beautiful. Her distinctive traits acknowledged an African-Asian ancestry. Her features were soft and delicate against her warm complexion. Her eyes were slight and angular and her nose whisper thin. Her cheeks were full and high with deep dimples, and she had the most perfect, most kissable lips of any woman in the room.

Her attire was conservative, a stark contradiction to the sultry gyrations that had the men in the room hovering around her like flies. Her loose, black cotton, button-up blouse and wide-legged slacks did nothing to flatter her figure. But with each shake of her hips a man could just imagine the lush curves and warm skin her clothes covered. As Zak found himself imagining, he couldn't stop himself from smiling.

Across the room Maitlyn had finally taken a seat at one of the front tables. Three men sat down beside her, each of them vying for her attention. Zak knew two of the men by name. Frank Barber was an attorney from New York City, and Gerard Bruner was a doctor from Zimbabwe. Both were opponents he'd be going up against in the poker tournament. The third man seemed most intent on diverting Maitlyn's full attention away from her other admirers. For a brief moment she seemed quite enamored with the blond-haired man, with his striking good looks and deep blue eyes. And then suddenly she didn't; something in her glass no longer fueled her fun.

Zak's radar suddenly engaged as he leaned forward in his seat. Although most of the room wasn't paying an ounce of attention, he sensed that something wasn't quite right as he closely observed the man who was pulling Maitlyn to her feet. Without giving it a second thought, Zak crossed the room in quick strides to where they'd been sitting.

"Ms. Boudreaux, can I be of some assistance?" he asked, cutting an eye at the man who had one arm around her waist and the other clutching her elbow.

Maitlyn shook her head from side to side. "I don't feel well," she murmured softly. Her eyes rolled skyward, her lashes fluttering.

"I've got this, thank you," her companion snapped as he moved to leave.

Zak took a step to block his path. "And you are?" he questioned, meeting the man's annoyed gaze.

"None of your business. My wife said she wasn't feeling well."

"Your wife?"

"Do you have a problem with that?"

The two men still seated at the table came to their feet. Frank Barber spoke first. "Mr. Sayed, it's good to see you."

Zak's gaze remained focused on Maitlyn's new friend. He didn't bother to respond.

"Mr. Lloyd, this is Zakaria Sayed. Mr. Sayed, this is Alexander Lloyd and the young woman is a friend of ours. She's not feeling well, and he was just helping her to her cabin."

Zak nodded ever so slightly. "Well, the young woman came on board with me, not Mr. Lloyd. And since she isn't married, I know that Mr. Lloyd can't possibly be her husband. And the fact that he lied makes me question his intent."

The blond-haired man bristled. "She's a very close friend."

"I don't feel so good," Maitlyn repeated again in a brief moment of lucidity.

"We appreciate your help, Mr. Lloyd, but I'll take her from here," Zak stated matter-of-factly.

"I can take her—" the man started.

Gerard Bruner interjected, cutting a stern eye at his friend. "Not a problem, Mr. Sayed. We were all just trying to be of some assistance."

Zak cast a brusque eye at the man, then gestured for

one of the cruise ship's employees. The man was at his elbow before he could even lower his arm.

"Yes, sir, Mr. Sayed. Is there a problem, sir?"

"Have the ship's doctor meet me in my suite, please. Ms. Boudreaux isn't feeling well," he said as he moved forward, gently pulling Maitlyn from the other man's grasp and sweeping her up into his arms. Instinctively she wrapped both of her arms around his neck and laid her head onto his broad chest.

"Yes, sir. Right away, sir," the man gushed as he hurried off.

The man introduced as Mr. Lloyd scowled. Zak looked from Bruner to Lloyd again, who looked down, nervously adjusting his collar. Without another word, Zak turned an about-face and carried Maitlyn out of the club.

The ship's doctor, his nurse and the cruise director were waiting at his door. Stacy's eyes widened with concern.

"Mr. Sayed, we can take Ms. Boudreaux down to the infirmary. You don't need to be bothered, sir."

"Did I say I was bothered?"

"I just— We—" she stuttered as Zak gestured for one of them to open the room's door.

After moving inside, he laid Maitlyn down gently onto the oversize sofa. She moaned softly. He couldn't resist brushing his fingers across her forehead, sweeping the length of her hair from her eyes. Her gaze briefly met his, and she struggled to smile.

"Has she taken anything?" the doctor asked as he moved in to examine her.

Zak shrugged. "I believe she's been drinking. I'm not aware of anything else," he answered.

The doctor nodded. "Do you mind if we move her upstairs to the bed?" he asked.

Zak shook his head and bent to lift her a second time. Without an ounce of effort he carried her up the short flight of stairs to the second level and laid her across the bed.

Maitlyn suddenly lurched forward, her torso rising as she reached her arms out to him. Dropping down against the bedside, Zak gently returned the embrace.

"The doctor's here. He'll make you feel better."

Nodding her head against his chest, Maitlyn purred softly and then heaved, vomiting down the front of Zak's gray silk suit.

Maitlyn's eyes snapped open. Her eyes skated around the room as she took in her surroundings. For a brief moment she didn't know where she was and then she remembered she was on a massive ship cruising across the Atlantic. The easy side-to-side sway of the bed she rested in was soothing. She noted that the space was luxurious, much nicer than her own cabin. And suddenly her anxiety returned—Maitlyn had no clue whose cabin, or bed, she was in.

She sat upright. The last thing she remembered was the nightclub and the intoxicating beat that had vibrated from the tips of her toes to the top of her head. She remembered the room full of revelers and dancing as if she didn't have a care in the world. Because for the first time since her trip had started, she hadn't. Not one. For the first time, in quite some time, she had been completely and totally content.

And then she remembered the table of men who had spent the first two days of her trip flattering her vanity with compliment after compliment as they'd lavished her with attention. Most especially Alexander Lloyd, the silver-tongued Englishman with the devilish blue eyes. Lloyd had been particularly attentive, and Maitlyn remembered thinking that she might not go to bed alone that night. After that, everything else was a complete and total blank.

As Maitlyn tried to remember the past few hours of her life, pondering how she'd come to be in someone else's bed, Zak Sayed stepped into the room, wearing nothing but a towel wrapped around his waist. Maitlyn's mouth dropped open as shock washed over her expression. She grabbed at the covers and pulled them beneath her chin. She suddenly felt quite naked in whatever it was she was wearing because she didn't have a clue if she had on clothes or not. She tossed a quick look beneath the blankets and spied the oversize T-shirt that she was clothed in. She didn't have on panties.

Zak stopped short. He tossed her a slight smile. "Good evening. You are finally awake."

She nodded as her eyes bulged wide. "How…how long have I been out?" she asked, suddenly having a ton of questions. "How did I get here? Where are my clothes? Did we—?"

Zak smiled easily, but the gesture did nothing to calm Maitlyn's nerves. The uneasy wave in the pit of her abdomen spun like a roller coaster out of control. She was suddenly focused on his magnanimous smile and his half-naked body. His broad chest was well-defined, showcasing picture-perfect six-pack abs. His skin was the color of rich, warm nutmeg and smooth like fine silk stretched over hardened steel. The muscular lines narrowed at his waistline, and she couldn't miss the hint of black hair that peeked over the front edge of the bright white towel that sat low around his hips. She could only imagine where that slight wisp of tight curl led beneath that towel. Her gaze shifted down to his legs; the limbs were long and unyielding like the trunk of a mighty tree. And his feet, like his hands, were large, a solid foundation holding him upright. She struggled not to stare so blatantly.

Still smiling, Zakaria responded, "Two days. You've been asleep since Tuesday. You had me worried for a moment but the doctor assured me you were fine."

"Tuesday? What happened to me?" she queried, finally lifting her eyes back to his.

"Your body needed rest and then you drank too much." His tone held a hint of judgment and his gaze was critical. Zak was not fond of women who could not hold their alcohol.

Maitlyn felt her body tense. She hesitated, shifting her eyes from side to side. "I didn't...I..." she stammered, finally finding the words. "I don't drink," she finally said.

Zak stared at her. "You were drinking rum punch."

She shook her head. "No. I was drinking punch but without the rum. I don't drink. I don't like how it makes me feel, and I would never risk losing control because I drank too much. I don't drink," she professed a second time. "Ever!"

Zak studied her momentarily. The look on her face was telling, and he appeared suddenly angry. He swallowed hard, bottling the emotion. He bit down against his bottom lip, then pursed his lips together, his jaw locked tight.

Maitlyn closely observed Zak, still trying to make sense of the moment.

"You were exhausted and dehydrated. I'm sure you hadn't eaten properly and when you did something obviously didn't agree with you," Zak finally replied. "Before you passed out, you vomited on your clothes and the nurse changed you. The doctor gave you two bags of IV fluids to flush and hydrate your system and then said to let you rest."

Maitlyn took a deep breath. "But how did I get here…in your room?"

"I promised your brother I would look out for you. I keep my promises."

For the first time Maitlyn returned his smile with one of her own. "Thank you."

Zak dipped his head. "Are you hungry? Do you think you can eat something?"

"I *am* hungry," she answered; the rumble in her stomach finally felt like a hunger pang. "And I feel fine… well rested actually."

"I can call for room service or you are welcome to join me in the dining room. Whichever you prefer?"

Maitlyn hesitated as she pondered her options. She finally nodded. "The dining room would be nice, I think."

"I'll get dressed downstairs. When you're ready, we can go to the dining room." Zak took a quick glance at the wristwatch he'd rested atop the dresser. "You'll need to hurry, though. The tournament starts later this evening, so I am limited on time."

"I don't have my clothes!" Maitlyn exclaimed, tightening the grip she had on the sheet clutched in her hands.

"Not to worry. Just take your shower," Zak stated as he moved out of the room.

When she heard the sound of a door opening and closing from the space below, she rose from the bed. She tossed back the covers and threw her legs off the side of the mattress. For a brief moment as she came to her feet, she felt as if she might fall; the room threatened to spin around her. Maitlyn took a deep breath and then a second, allowing the sensation to pass before she stood completely upright and headed into the bathroom.

"Wow!" Maitlyn exclaimed, taking in the expanse of space with its polished marble and gold-appointed treatments. Zak's accommodations had come with some serious perks, she thought. She crossed the heated floor to the tiled shower and turned on the faucet.

Minutes later Maitlyn stepped out of the spray of hot water and wrapped her own white towel around her body. Barely opening the bathroom door she peeked out into the bedroom space. Zakaria was nowhere to be found, but her luggage and personal belongings rested atop the bed. Maitlyn was still confused but determined to unravel the mystery of the past forty-eight hours. Almost a week of her trip had passed and she couldn't remember a large part of it. None of it made any sense to her.

Zak suddenly called her name from the bottom of the stairwell. "I need to step out for a quick minute, but I'll be right back. They are holding our table so as soon as you are ready we can head to the dining room." His tone was warm and easy like thick, rich honey being spread on dark toast. His seductive cadence caused a shiver of heat to ripple through her feminine spirit. Taking a deep breath, Maitlyn clenched her pelvic muscles, contracting and relaxing the tissue until the feeling passed.

In no time at all she was dressed in a formfitting black knit dress and fire-engine-red pumps. She brushed a faint layer of mineral powdered foundation across her face, lined her eyes with black eyeliner and patted a tissue over the lipstick that brightened her lips. She pulled her fingers through the length of her hair, pulling the strands into a loose ponytail atop her head. When she was satisfied with the reflection staring back at her from the mirror, she headed down the stairs to the living space below, where Zak, back from his errand, stood patiently waiting for her.

As Maitlyn eased down the stairs, Zak's eyes widened with appreciation.

As they headed in the direction of the elevators, they crossed paths with Gerard and Frank. Both men voiced their concern for her health, seemingly interested in her well-being. Maitlyn was polite as she expressed her gratitude for their kind words. She stepped into Zak's side, leaning her body toward his. As the elevator stopped before them, Zak rested a possessive hand against her lower back and guided her into the conveyor. Taking the hint, Gerard and Frank gave them both a casual wave, opting to walk the stairs instead.

When the doors closed Maitlyn stepped away from Zak's touch and turned to face him. She stared up into his eyes. "I think someone drugged me," she stated, her voice a loud whisper. "One of them or that other man, their friend Alexander Lloyd."

Zak returned her intense look. "I thought he was your friend, too. That Lloyd guy?"

She shrugged, her brow creasing in thought. "I

thought he was nice. When we first met, he tried to buy me a drink, but I turned him down. I told him I don't drink, and he was very nice about it. He seemed… well…I…" She trailed off, not wanting Zak to think that there had ever been anything between her and the cute blond man. "I just don't know him like that," she finally sputtered.

Zak studied her for a brief moment, his gaze soothing.

Then a stray strand of hair fell over her eye, and he brushed it from her face with the tips of his fingers. As he did, she leaned her forehead into his palm and closed her eyes. The gesture felt intimate and both felt the air between them catch deep in their chests; oxygen suddenly felt like a precious commodity.

"I'll take care of it," Zak finally said, his head bobbing gently against his broad shoulders. As the doors opened, he stepped out ahead of her and hesitated. After turning an about-face, Zak extended his hand in her direction. In that moment Maitlyn instinctively trusted that if any man could right all the wrongs in the world, Zak Sayed would. After reaching her hand toward him, she entwined her fingers between his. And when he smiled, Maitlyn melted beneath the sheer beauty of it.

Chapter 4

Maitlyn laughed as Zak hit the punch line of the story he'd been telling her. Her joyous expression moved Zak to laugh along with her. He lifted his wineglass and took a sip of the Riesling he'd paired with his salmon entrée. Before he could drop the crystal goblet back to the table, their waiter was at his elbow refilling his glass.

"Thank you, Henry," Zak said.

The young man nodded. "And you, madam? Would you like more water?"

"No, thank you," Maitlyn answered. "I am full."

"Are you sure?" Zak pressed. "Coffee, tea, more dessert?"

Maitlyn giggled, pressing her palm against her abdomen. "Really, I couldn't eat another bite without getting sick again."

"Well, we definitely don't want you sick again," Zak said in agreement. "I like this suit!"

Maitlyn's eyes widened. "Please don't tell me I got sick on your suit."

Zak leaned back in his seat and crossed his hands together in his lap. He smiled brightly, his eyes gleaming.

Maitlyn persisted. "Did I? I didn't, did I?"

"You asked me not to tell you."

"Damn," Maitlyn exclaimed, heat rising to her cheeks. "I am so sorry!" Mortified, she pressed her hands over her face.

"Nothing to be embarrassed about. Those things happen."

"Not to me! Nothing like that has ever happened to me," Maitlyn said. "I will pay for your suit. And again, I am so sorry."

He shook his head. "Not to worry. My suit and your pretty blouse have been cleaned, pressed and returned to us. All's well again."

Maitlyn shook her head vehemently. "I bet you didn't bargain on any of this when you ran into my brother, did you?"

Zak laughed heartily. "Actually, with your brother I have to be ready for almost anything."

"You never told me how you two actually became acquainted."

"A business deal brought us together."

"What kind of deal?"

"A very lucrative one."

Maitlyn paused, eyeing the smirk on Zak's handsome face. "You aren't going to give me any details, are you?"

Zak looked down at the gold watch on his wrist. "I need to head to the casino. Will you be joining me?"

Maitlyn laughed. "You must drive your wife crazy," she said, the statement more inquisitive than a comment.

"I've never been married, actually."

"Your girlfriend, then."

Zak shrugged. "No, I don't have one of those, either. And no time, or desire, to drive anyone crazy." He leaned forward in his seat. "Now, will you be joining me?" he asked a second time, his eyes piercing hers.

"I'd like that," Maitlyn answered. "As long as I won't be in the way."

Zak came to his feet, dropping the cloth napkin in his lap onto the table. "If you were going to be in the way, Ms. Boudreaux, I would never have invited you."

Maitlyn's eyes were wide with wonder as she and Zak entered the ship's casino. The crowd that had gathered moved out of the way to make a path for Zakaria. Without blinking an eye, he slid his arm around her waist and guided her through the throng of people toward the casino manager, who greeted him warmly.

"Mr. Sayed, sir, what an honor it is to have you back with us!"

"It's a pleasure to be back, Mr. Turner."

The man cut an easy eye toward Maitlyn and smiled. Zak introduced her. "This is Ms. Boudreaux, and she'll be my personal guest for the duration of the cruise. Will you please ensure that she's comfortable?"

"Most certainly, sir," Mr. Turner said as he gestured toward Maitlyn. "Ms. Boudreaux, if you'll follow me, please."

Zak caught her eye and nodded, saying nothing as he turned and moved in the direction of the gaming table.

Maitlyn followed Mr. Turner to a booth that sat one level above the center of the room. She had a front-row view of the tables and the games below. He pulled out the chair for her to sit, his smile still wide in his round face. "Would you like a drink?" he questioned. "The bar is complimentary for players and their guests."

She shook her head. "No. Thank you. But if I can, a cup of coffee, please?"

Mr. Turner nodded. "I'll have that brought right over," he said.

Maitlyn nodded her appreciation as the man turned and headed in the opposite direction. She focused her attention on the activity in the center of the room. The players were just beginning to take their seats. There were six tables with six players each. Zak stood beside a table with Gerard, three other men and a woman Maitlyn recognized from the ship's jewelry store days earlier. He eased his suit jacket off his shoulders and claimed his chair, tossing his jacket over the chair's back.

Gerard's friend Frank was seated at another table and Alexander Lloyd at a third. Both Gerard and Frank waved in her direction. Alexander barely lifted an eye to acknowledge her, instead looking past her as if she weren't even in the room. A petite young woman who looked half his age was hanging on his arm, intent on keeping his full and undivided attention.

A tall redhead brought over Maitlyn's coffee. "Ms. Boudreaux, your beverage," the young woman said as she set a silver tray down onto the table and proceeded to pour Maitlyn's coffee into a ceramic mug. "Cream and sugar, ma'am?"

"Thank you," Maitlyn said, her eyes still skating around the room.

"Is this your first tournament?" the woman asked.

Maitlyn nodded, lifting her gaze to the woman who was eyeing her curiously. The name tag on the woman's uniform read Lourdes.

"Is it that obvious?" Maitlyn asked.

Lourdes smiled. "Usually the women who sit in the players' boxes all look bored to death. You look excited."

Maitlyn laughed. "I guess I am. I didn't realize it was going to be this big. Or this involved." She looked back to all the activity on the level below.

"The World Series of Poker tour is the most prestigious series of poker tournaments. But this is the tournament above all other tournaments," Lourdes noted. "These are the top players and winners from all over the world. It's by invitation only and they still have to pay ten million dollars to buy into the game. They're playing Texas Hold'em, with no limit. The pots will be extremely big and the winner will take home two hundred and fifty million dollars when it's all done."

"Ten million dollars just to play?" Maitlyn's head snapped back as she turned to stare at the woman, her eyes blinking rapidly. Her expression was incredulous. "Are you kidding me?"

Lourdes shook her head. "I'm dead serious. It cost your boyfriend a pretty penny to have a seat in this game. But if he wins, he gets that back and then some!"

"Oh, he's not my—" she started, when the two were suddenly interrupted by Zak, who had eased to her side.

"Am I interrupting?" he asked as he sat down beside her.

"No, not at all," Maitlyn answered. She cut an eye at Lourdes, who was still smiling brightly, unfazed by the man's presence.

"Is there anything I can get you, Mr. Sayed?" Lourdes questioned. The silver tray was perched easily in her left hand while her right was pulled back against the small of her back.

He nodded. "I'm drinking Scotch tonight, Lourdes. Neat. Please make sure my glass stays full at all times. When I've had enough I'll let you know. You won't need to ask me about refills."

"Yes, sir." Lourdes nodded. "Will there be anything else, sir?"

He shook his head. "Please make sure Ms. Boudreaux has anything her heart desires."

"Yes, sir, Mr. Sayed."

With a nod of his head, Zak dismissed the woman. She waved an easy hand at Maitlyn, then turned and headed in the direction of the bar.

"I just wanted to make sure you were well before we started," he said, turning his attention toward her.

"Actually, I'm a little overwhelmed," she said.

Zak smiled. "I can understand that. Hopefully you'll find it entertaining."

"I already do," Maitlyn said, smiling back.

He got back to his feet. "We break periodically, so I'll check on you when I can," he said as he pulled his suit jacket closed around his torso and moved to leave.

Maitlyn called after him.

"Yes?"

"Good luck," she said, her smile a mile wide.

Zak smiled back, tossing her an easy nod as he turned and sauntered back to his seat at the gaming table.

An hour later, as Maitlyn watched she couldn't help but think that luck would have absolutely nothing to do with his success. Clearly, this game was going to take some serious skill.

Although she had never played poker before, Maitlyn understood the mechanics of the game enough to quickly catch on. Unlike other card games, Texas Hold'em was a game of risk that forced players to rely on strategy, skill and patience.

She was impressed with Zakaria's acumen. The man's nonchalant demeanor made for the perfect game face. He never once broke a sweat, even when Maitlyn sensed that the play wasn't going in his favor. With the impressive amounts of money being waged, Maitlyn knew that if she were playing she would have broken a sweat and then some.

Occasionally Zak lifted his eyes to look in her direction, but his facial expression never changed. He always seemed fully focused on the cards in his hand and very little else. A few of his opponents were far less reserved; one even jumped up and down and screamed like a banshee when he lost his hand and, apparently, his life savings.

It was shortly after midnight when the first round of play was done, and twenty-four of the original players had advanced to the next round. Zak bypassed the congratulatory handshaking and made his way back to her side. He eased into the seat across from her and reached for the fresh drink Lourdes has deposited on the table seconds earlier. Without realizing it, Maitlyn had kept track, noting that he'd actually only had one drink the entire evening, having sipped it slowly while he played. The one in his hand was his second, and he downed it quickly. Lourdes was there with a refill before either of them could blink. She winked at Maitlyn before she moved away.

"I overheard someone talking, and they said you won this tournament last year," Maitlyn said, breaking the silence between them.

Zak nodded, his gaze skating around the room. "I did."

"Wow! I just can't imagine risking that kind of money on a card game."

He cut a quick eye in her direction. "You take a risk when you get up in the morning and walk out your door. Life is a risk. I choose to live well and have been fortunate to be able to pick and choose my challenges. This *card game* is about much more than the money for me. And I only gamble what I can easily afford to just give away."

Maitlyn sensed that she had struck a nerve. His tone indicated that her comment might have offended him, and she immediately apologized.

"I've always been very prudent about everything in my life, particularly my money. I could never be that daring. I admire your boldness."

Zak turned to stare at her. "To be honest, I didn't take you for being an overly cautious woman. You're traveling alone. I think it takes a very daring spirit to do something like that, especially outside the United States. Other countries are not so approving of such a thing."

Maitlyn laughed. "I didn't have much say in the matter," she said, telling him about her divorce and explaining how she'd come to be on the ship by her lonesome.

When she was done telling her story, Zak nodded. "Well hopefully," he said as he leaned in toward her, lifting his glass in salute, "this trip will be everything you want it to be."

Maitlyn lifted her coffee cup. "I'm keeping my fingers crossed," she said.

The two sat together in deep conversation for another hour. The ease of it surprised Maitlyn. She was surprised that she was enjoying his company as much as she was and also that Zak seemed genuinely interested in getting to know her.

Suddenly, they were interrupted by a woman calling Zak's name. Both turned at the same time to see who was quickly moving toward them. The young woman was stunning, tall and sleek with skin the color of dark mahogany, eyes like saucers and a full, red-lipped pout. Moving to his feet, Zak smiled brightly as he pulled her into a deep hug.

"Zakaria Sayed!" the girl gushed. "What a surprise!"

Zak brilliant smile was as wide as the ocean. "Izabella! It's good to see you!"

"You're here to keep your title, I see."

He chuckled softly, not bothering to answer.

She nodded and then shifted her eye toward Maitlyn. Her smile was curious as she introduced herself. "Hello, my name is Izabella. Zak and I are old friends."

Maitlyn recognized the world-famous Brazilian supermodel. "It's a pleasure to meet you. I'm Maitlyn Boudreaux. Zak and I are new friends."

Izabella tilted her head slightly. "Are you by chance related to Kendrick and Guy Boudreaux?"

Maitlyn nodded. "You know my brothers?"

Izabella giggled, her smile widening. "Guy and I did a fashion shoot together for Giorgio Armani last year. His wife and your brother Kendrick were in Naples with him. We all had a wonderful time together!"

"It's a small world," Maitlyn said.

Zak gestured for Izabella to take a seat and join them. "So what brings you on this cruise, Izabella?" he asked as she slid into the seat beside him.

Izabella paused as Lourdes suddenly appeared with a refill for Zak and a glass of champagne for her. She continued once the waitress had returned to her station. "I've been traveling with my father. He thought this would be a nice break for the two of us. Plus, you know how much he loves the casinos. He keeps hoping he'll strike it big at the blackjack table." Izabella rolled her eyes. She took a breath before continuing. "I'll be getting off in Greece, though. I have a photo shoot there, and right after that I fly to London to prep for Fashion Week."

Maitlyn sat back as the two old friends caught up with each other. She was amazed at Izabella's bubbly enthusiasm. The young woman talked nonstop, and her exuberance had a childlike quality. Izabella actually reminded her of her baby sister, Tarah. Maitlyn found herself curious to know more about her and Kendrick because Izabella Barros seemed very smitten with her brother's friend Zak.

Maitlyn watched as the woman's hands danced across Zak's chest and caressed his arms. Her touchy-feely manner shifted Maitlyn out of the quiet ambiance she'd been enjoying with Zak and she suddenly felt like the third wheel. When it became too much for her, she feigned a yawn, drawing a palm to cover her mouth. "Excuse me," she exclaimed, color rising to her cheeks.

Zak smiled that generous smile of his. "I imagine you're tired. Maybe you should go get some rest?"

Maitlyn nodded. "I am, and I should," she said as she came to her feet and extended a hand in Zak's direction. "Thank you. I really appreciate everything you've done for me."

Zak nodded. "I can walk you—"

She shook her head. "That's not necessary, but I appreciate the offer." She turned toward Izabella. "It was very nice to meet you."

"Let's plan on spending time together," Izabella said. "I'd love to talk to you more."

Maitlyn nodded. "Definitely! Well, enjoy the rest of your evening."

At the entrance to the casino, Maitlyn turned back to take one last look. The room was clouded. Cigarette smoke had formed a veiled screen throughout the space. Across the way Zak and Izabella were huddled comfortably together, lost in conversation. Jealousy suddenly rippled with a vengeance as she turned and headed from the room.

Minutes later Maitlyn stood in front of her cabin's door, looking completely lost. She couldn't begin to remember where she'd left the key card that gained her entry. She looked down the hallway—the corridor was empty. As she pondered her options, she realized that even if she did get into her own room all her personal possessions were still in Zak's suite. She shook her head at the conundrum.

This can't be happening to me, Maitlyn thought, feeling completely out of control. *Okay,* she thought, as she reasoned what to do. *It really isn't a problem, is it?* Obviously she was going to have to disturb Zak. If he was still in the casino, she could just make her way back there and ask for help. But what if he wasn't? What if he and his old friend Izabella were together someplace else?

Maitlyn sighed deeply. She couldn't begin to explain why it bothered her that Zak might still be with that woman. But it did, and if he was, she really didn't want to know. Taking a deep breath, Maitlyn crossed her fingers and wished a prayer skyward. With any luck Zak was still right where she'd left him. And maybe if luck was on her side, Izabella would be gone.

Chapter 5

"You always get the best accommodations!" Izabella gushed as she explored Zak's suite.

Zak laughed, pulling at his necktie as he dropped down onto the living room sofa. The young woman moved to his side, then stood in front of him. She leaned forward, undid his necktie completely and tossed it on the floor behind him. Standing tall, she gave him a teasing smile. Zak watched as she slowly undid the halter top of the jumpsuit she wore. The garment fell to the floor. She struck a pose in nothing but her lace G-string and her five-inch pumps. Her breasts were small, the size of tennis balls, and she was so thin that she appeared almost fragile. But she had just enough curve to her hips and ass to capture a man's attention, and her legs were miles long.

But she didn't have Zak's attention, and if she had not been so self-absorbed, she would have seen it in the look he was giving her. If Izabella had been paying an ounce of attention, she would have seen that Zak was still thinking of Maitlyn; thoughts of the beautiful woman had consumed him ever since she had left his side.

"What are you doing, Izabella?" he finally asked as he leaned back in his seat and stretched his arms out across the sofa's cushioned top.

She smiled. "Making myself comfortable," she giggled as she stepped out of the lace fabric. She did a quick pirouette, then moved toward the stairs and headed to the second floor. "This is too sweet!" she called down to the level below.

Zak shook his head. He and Izabella had history. They'd been friends since he'd met her ten years ago when her modeling career was just beginning to take off. She'd gotten herself tangled up with an unsavory photographer, and her father had employed him to retrieve some compromising photographs of the girl.

Occasionally, when she didn't have a boyfriend, she warmed his bed. But Izabella liked having a boyfriend, most especially one she could manipulate. She had never been able to manipulate Zak, and he appreciated that she never expected more from him than what he was willing to offer. Izabella was not a woman he could ever take seriously, and so he'd given her very little of himself. Their relationship had been purely physical, and Zak preferred it that way. It worked for the two of them even when it shouldn't have.

Izabella had insisted on following him back to his room, and he'd let her. But once he'd closed the door, he found himself wishing he'd told her no. He had no desire to spend the night with the girl, and letting her in had given her reason to think that he did. He could only think of one woman he was interested in sharing his bed, and she wasn't there. He couldn't help but wonder if Maitlyn was thinking of him, too.

Izabella suddenly bounced back down the stairs. "Why didn't you tell me your lady friend was staying with you?"

"Excuse me?"

She pointed to the second floor. "Kendrick's sister. You should have told me she was staying here with you."

Zak's eyes widened. He'd completely forgotten that Maitlyn's luggage was still upstairs in his bedroom. He was suddenly concerned with where she was and if she'd been able to get into her own room. Just as he moved to his feet, intent on searching her out, there was a knock at his door. With quick strides he moved to the entrance and pulled it open. Maitlyn stood sheepishly on the other side.

"Hey, I'm sorry to bother you but—" she started, and then she caught sight of a very naked Izabella standing in the room behind him. Embarrassment flushed her face a deep shade of red. "I'm interrupting," Maitlyn stammered as she took a step back. "I didn't mean—"

Zak opened the door wider. "You're not. Please, come in," he said nonchalantly. "Izabella was just leaving."

Izabella waved a lazy hand in her direction. "I guess I am leaving," the woman said as she stepped back into her clothing and tied the garment around her neck. She laughed easily as she rolled her eyes. After moving to the door, she reached up to press a kiss on Zak's cheek. "Why don't we all meet for breakfast in the morning? Papa will love to see you, Zakaria," she said.

Zak nodded his agreement. "We will call you," he answered, and Izabella spun on her high heels and headed down the corridor.

Shock still painting her expression, Maitlyn met Zak's intense gaze. His head slightly tilted toward her. "My apology," he said as he gestured for her to enter the room.

"I really didn't mean to interrupt," she said, still not moving past the entrance.

"You weren't," Zak answered.

"You had a high-profile supermodel standing naked in your room. I find it hard to believe that I didn't just interrupt something."

Zak shrugged his broad shoulders. "I don't know why. I would think by now that you would know I'm not a man who says things I don't mean."

"But she *was* naked."

Zak smiled. "Are you coming in, or do you plan to stand out there all night?"

Maitlyn forced a smile. "My luggage is still here."

"I know," he said, still staring at her. The two held the gaze for a few moments before Zak finally turned his back to her and moved inside. He reclaimed his seat on the sofa.

Maitlyn hesitated for a brief moment before she followed and entered the room, closing the door behind her. She paused and stood awkwardly when she reached the couch, and Zak stared at her intently.

"Are you and Izabella lovers?" she blurted out before she could catch the words.

He smiled. "We have been," he answered emotionlessly. "We are not anymore, nor do I expect that we will ever be again in the future. Is that a problem for you?"

She shook her head. "No, why would it be a problem for me? I was just curious. You two just seem very comfortable with each other."

He shrugged. "I had to assist Izabella's father with getting her out of a situation a few years ago. We were close and then we weren't." Zak smiled again. He continued to stare at her. His appreciative gaze roved over the lines of her body. The room suddenly felt warm; heat rose with a vengeance.

Zak pointed to the empty chair, gesturing for her to take a seat. "So come tell me why you are so curious about the women I might have made love to," he said.

She hesitated for a brief moment, then moved to where he pointed. She took a seat and crossed one lean leg over the other. "I was only curious about Izabella," she finally answered. "Your personal life is none of my business."

Zak was still staring at her legs. She had runner's legs, tight, toned and muscular. He was suddenly imagining himself lost deep between her thighs, and the notion caused a wave of heat to simmer between his legs. He forced himself to lift his gaze from her legs back to her face. There was something in her eyes that he found engaging, and her seductive gaze hinted at her own desires. Maitlyn Boudreaux was a beautiful woman, but there was something more there that he found himself attracted to.

When they locked eyes, Maitlyn gasped and bit down against her bottom lip.

"You should get some rest," he said finally. "You are welcome to spend the night here. I'll sleep down here on the sofa bed."

"I really shouldn't," she stated. "I can just get my things and…"

There was a moment of hesitation before Zak moved swiftly to his feet. His tone was easy and gentle, his statement uttered easily. "I don't want you to leave," he said. "I think you should just rest tonight. We will worry about moving you tomorrow." He strode to the balcony doors and slid them open. "Sleep well, my friend." He tossed her a quick look over his shoulder before stepping outside and closing the door behind him.

Zak turned to watch Maitlyn head up the stairs to the second floor and to his bed.

Hours later, Zak woke to the distinctive smell of ocean air and a bouquet of sea salt teasing his nostrils. He stretched his body upward, elongating his limbs against the cushions of the teak lounger. It had not been his intent to fall asleep outside on the deck, but he had needed to keep some distance between himself and Maitlyn. It had taken much for him not to climb those stairs behind her and even more to regain control over his body.

Those last moments with Maitlyn had been a test of his fortitude. As he'd watched her, her eyes wide with longing and her lips quivering with want, the sultry expression that had painted her face had hardened every muscle in his body. It had taken everything in him not to ravage her right there where she stood. The chilly night air had served to ease the rise of tension, but every time he thought about going back inside, his body betrayed him as he imagined her upstairs in his bed. He stood up and leaned over the railing, looking out to the expanse of water that dressed the landscape. The sun was just beginning to rise in the distance ahead.

They had been cruising for one week straight, and it would be one more day before they saw land again. The first port of call was Funchal, on the island of Madeira. It was a popular year-round resort that had become a major harbor for cruise line dockings and he anticipated that they would be able to see the shoreline in the wee hours of the following morning.

As he moved back into the cabin, the phone on the desk began to ring. Shaking his head, Zak knew who was calling even before he answered. "Yes, Izabella?"

"Are we still doing breakfast?" the young woman chimed, sounding far too chipper for the early morning hour.

"I thought I said I would call you," Zak said.

"Papa gets up early. Much too early for me, but since this is his trip I'm trying to be the dutiful daughter. Now you and Maitlyn come save me!" Izabella exclaimed.

"Maitlyn is still resting."

"Roll over and wake her up, then meet us in the dining room in an hour."

"You know, you sometimes go too far, Izabella," Zak stated, bristling at her comment.

"Oh, don't be a party pooper! I'm starting to get claustrophobic on this boat, and I just want to have some fun. Plus, I want to get to know Maitlyn better. I saw how you were looking at her, Zakaria!"

"Again, too far," he responded. "And you didn't see any such thing."

"I saw enough. Now are you coming? Papa is here and wants to know."

Zak sighed. "Tell your father that Maitlyn and I will meet you in an hour," he answered just before disconnecting the call.

After easing up the stairwell, Zak found Maitlyn still sound asleep. Just as he'd done for the past two days, he stood staring down at her for a brief moment before moving into the bathroom to shower. Unlike those previous two days, Maitlyn had tossed off all the covers, and her body was pressed facedown against the mattress. Zak was taken aback by the view.

The beautiful woman was wearing very little, nothing but a tank top and bikini bottoms that barely covered the roundness of her derriere. The legs he'd admired the previous night were sprawled open, wide and inviting. The curve of her buttocks was lush and full, and Zak licked his lips as he admired the view. Fantasizing how her backside might feel in his hands lengthened an erection in his pants. The length of steel between his legs was desperate for attention. Resisting the urge to touch her, and himself, he turned and moved into the bathroom to take a very cold shower.

Behind the closed bathroom door, he leaned on the granite counters, his hands clenched in fists as he rested his weight on his arms. His muscles bulged as he leaned into the mirror, staring at his reflection. The temptation was more than he'd anticipated. But he couldn't afford to let his rising desire for the woman distract him from what he needed to do. And despite Maitlyn becoming a serious distraction, what he needed most was to stay focused.

She heard the water running in the other room; the lull of it pulled her from a deep sleep. There was a chill in the air, and Maitlyn was suddenly cold. She reached for the blankets that were tangled at her feet. As she pulled the bedclothes up and over her body, she couldn't help but wonder what Zak might have seen as he'd passed on his way to the bathroom. She rolled onto her back and pulled an arm up and over her eyes.

Obviously, the man had gotten an eyeful, she told herself. She should have been bothered by that, she thought, but she wasn't. And although she hoped he liked what he'd seen, she couldn't help but wonder if Zak had compared her to that naked twenty-eight-year-old who'd been offering him her treats just before Maitlyn had shown up at his door. She couldn't help but wonder if he might have been disappointed. She blew out a deep sigh, her head waving from side to side.

Admittedly, her confidence was shaken. She had tossed and turned for most of the night, mindful that Zak was only steps away from her. She'd been more than tempted to call him up to her and had even fantasized about easing back down the stairs to his side, doing a seductive striptease with each step. She couldn't begin to understand what had gotten into her—her desire was like a fungus spreading out of control. She had wanted nothing more than to throw herself at him, but the fear of rejection had kept her at bay.

But something about Zakaria Sayed had teased every one of her sensibilities. Weeks ago, prim and proper Maitlyn wouldn't have had an interest in any man and definitely not a man who had her ready to strip right out of her panties. But Maitlyn was suddenly very interested in Zak and there was nothing prim or proper about the thoughts she was having about him.

When the sound of the shower stalled, Maitlyn rolled onto her side, pulling the covers tighter around her body. As Zak moved about in the other room, she pondered ways to get his attention, thinking that she just might throw caution to the wind and tell him what she was feeling. As the bathroom door swung open, she closed her eyes tight, feigning sleep. She could feel Zak staring down at her, and she clenched her knees tightly together beneath the covers. Zak called her name once and then a second time as he rounded the bed, moving to her side.

"Maitlyn, are you awake?" he asked, his tone low.

Maitlyn eased her eyes open, willing a smile onto her face. "Just dozing," she murmured. "Good morning."

Zak was bare chested, nothing covering him but a towel. "Good morning. Izabella and her father called about breakfast. I told them we'd meet them in the dining room in an hour. I hope that was okay?"

She took a deep breath. "Oh, yeah, that's fine."

Zak nodded, still staring down at her. Maitlyn met his gaze, her own eyes wide as she struggled not to focus on his broad chest or the slight tent that had lifted in the front of his towel. But he was staring, and the look he was giving her had hardened her nipples and made her moist between her thighs.

Maitlyn cleared her throat. "Why are you looking at me like that?" she questioned.

"You're an incredibly beautiful woman. I can't help myself," he said, his eyes skating easily over her profile.

Butterflies fluttered in her midsection. She smiled sweetly. "Thank you."

"I'll be downstairs," he said as he took two steps back and turned away from her.

Maitlyn sat upright in the bed and called after him. "Zak!"

As he turned toward her, his broad chest throbbed up and down. "Yes?"

Maitlyn locked eyes with him, every thought she'd had moments earlier leaving her. She took a deep breath and then a second as she shook her head. "It's nothing," she finally muttered, her face flushed.

Zak paused briefly, and then he turned and moved quickly back down the stairs.

Chapter 6

Gustavo Barros talked as much and as fast as his daughter. Maitlyn slowly shook her head. Breakfast with the duo had been like an extreme tennis match, the back-and-forth exchange a challenge to follow. Maitlyn cut an eye toward Zak, who seemed oblivious, having tuned the two out an hour earlier. Izabella was regaling them with details of her trip to South Africa, and her father interjected his opinion about her less than stellar behavior.

"It's time you settled down," Gustavo exclaimed.

Izabella rolled her eyes. "I am too young to settle down, Papa! Tell him, Zak. He will not listen to me."

"It's you who should be doing the listening, Izabella. Your father is telling you well, but your head is hard."

The girl fanned a dismissive hand at him. "What do you think, Maitlyn? Should I not be enjoying myself? I am still young!"

Maitlyn smiled. "I think your father just wants to know that you are safe when you are out of his eyesight," she said. "I don't think he wants to stop you from having fun."

"I can't tell," Izabella responded. She quickly changed the subject. "So what do you two have planned for today?" she asked, looking from Maitlyn to Zak.

Zak leaned forward in his seat. "I've made plans for Maitlyn and I to spend time alone together this afternoon. Then of course there is the tournament tonight," he said.

A wide smile pulled at Izabella's face. "Alone!" she cooed. "That sounds intriguing!"

Gustavo laughed. "Which means that it is none of your business." The man rose to his feet. He extended a hand toward Zak. "Zakaria, it was good to see you again. Perhaps we'll have dinner together before we dock in Greece."

"Maitlyn and I look forward to it," Zak answered.

Gustavo leaned down to kiss Maitlyn's left cheek and then her right. "It was a pleasure to meet you, Maitlyn. Continue to enjoy your cruise."

"It was nice to meet you, too!" Maitlyn said with a smile.

Gustavo turned toward his daughter. "Izabella, I want to do the rock climbing on that wall at the far end of this boat. Are you ready?"

Izabella pouted. "Rock climbing? Really, Father? Do I have to?"

Zak cleared his throat. "Obey your father, Izabella," he said sternly.

The young woman heaved a deep sigh as she stood up. "I may watch, but I'm not doing anything that might ruin my manicure. I'll see you tonight at the tournament," she said as she followed after her father.

Zak chuckled softly as the two disappeared from view.

"Well," Maitlyn said, shaking her head. "That was interesting."

Zak nodded his agreement. "*Interesting* is one word you could use to describe them. I have others."

Maitlyn laughed.

Zak took a quick glance at his wristwatch. "We should be going ourselves," he said.

Maitlyn eyed him curiously. "Where? I didn't think you really meant that we were going to spend the afternoon together. I thought you were just saying that to get rid of Izabella."

Zak shook his head. He crossed his hands together on the table in front of him, his eyes connecting with hers. "Why would I say something I didn't mean?" he asked her.

"Because you're a man, and it's been my experience that's what men do," she answered, meaning every word.

Zak paused for a brief moment as he considered her words. He finally nodded and then spoke. "Clearly, you've spent too much time with the wrong man."

She shrugged. She thoroughly agreed with him, but she didn't say so out loud. Zak was still looking at her as if he expected her to say something, but she didn't bother to speak, just shrugged her shoulders a second time.

He spoke instead. "I'm a man of my word, Maitlyn, and I never say anything I do not mean. Know that," he said, his tone emphatic. "Now, if I overstepped my bounds thinking that you might want to spend the afternoon with me, please let me know. In which case I will apologize and you can be on your way."

She shook her head, feeling a little shell-shocked by his virility. Other than her brothers, it had been a good long while since she'd been in the company of a man who didn't have a problem showing just how much of a man he was. Zakaria had monumental presence, and she was feeling every ounce of it. "I would love to spend the afternoon with you," she finally said.

Zak nodded and smiled. "They're waiting for us." He stood up and extended his hand toward her. "Shall we?"

As they made their way to the opposite end of the ship, they happened on Frank, Gerard and Alexander Lloyd standing in a heated exchange. None of the men looked happy; Lloyd appeared particularly disturbed. The trio's conversation came to an abrupt halt when they caught sight of Zak and Maitlyn.

Gerard spoke first. "Mr. Sayed. Ms. Boudreaux, how are you?" he said, cutting a nervous eye at the other two men.

"I'm well. Thank you for asking," Maitlyn replied.

Zak nodded his head slightly, not bothering to respond.

"You played an impressive game last night, Mr. Sayed," Frank said. "You're the favorite to win again this year."

Zak was still silent, his posture a tad tense. The moment was awkward at best. Maitlyn looked from him to the others, noting that Lloyd hadn't bothered to look in their direction.

"How did you do?" she asked, hoping to ease some of the tension.

Frank tossed his hands up as if he were surrendering. "I'm sure I'll have better luck next year," he said. He gave her a nervous smile.

"How about you, Mr. Lloyd? Did you have a good night?" she questioned.

Alexander turned slightly in her direction. There was no missing the bruise that blackened his eye and the side of his face. Maitlyn's eyes widened at the sight.

Before she could ask what happened, the man made an abrupt exit.

"Well, that was rude," she exclaimed.

Gerard chuckled ever so slightly. "He's a little sensitive. He's playing again tonight, though."

Zak pressed a warm hand to her elbow. "We have to be going," he said firmly.

Maitlyn nodded. "You gentlemen have a nice day," she said as they eased past the other two and continued toward their destination. When they were out of earshot, she tossed Zak a quick look. "What do you think that was all about? Alexander was extremely rude, and did you see his face?"

"It's what happens when a man oversteps his bounds."

"He could have spoken, at least," she said.

Zak gave her a look. "Not if he knows what's good for him. He knows better than to say two words to you for the rest of this trip."

"What do you mean—" she started.

Zak held up his index finger. "Don't concern yourself with any of those men. I assure you they won't cause you any problems. I made sure of that."

Maitlyn met the look he was giving her. There was something in his eyes that gave her an understanding that he'd come through on his promise to take care of things. That knowledge both flattered and frightened her.

Minutes later Maitlyn was buck naked beneath a plush terry robe embroidered with the cruise line's logo. Standing in the center of the ship's spa, she was nervous and excited. Zak had scheduled a massage for the two of them. A *couple's* massage. He entered the space just minutes behind her, naked beneath his own robe.

After moving behind her, he dropped both his hands against her shoulders. As she tilted her head to stare up at him, he gave a quick wink of his eye and one of his bright smiles. Maitlyn suddenly felt like someone had lit a flame deep in the center of her core, setting her afire. It was almost more than she could bear and she found herself wishing she'd taken the glass of champagne that had been offered when they'd first arrived. She took a deep breath and held it, her eyes skating around to stare at anything other than him.

Soon a nice young woman led them to a private terrace. Overhead, the sky was a brilliant shade of blue, and large puffs of white clouds danced against the backdrop. The terrace was decorated with a bevy of tropical plants, and the sound of water trickled beneath soft music. Two massage therapists stood waiting: a tall young man with bleached blond hair and a young woman who reminded her of the actress Charlize Theron. The girl introduced herself and gestured for Maitlyn to follow her to a table. She held up an oversize sheet and Maitlyn stepped behind it, turning her back to Zak as she dropped her robe and lay down on her stomach. The woman draped the sheet over Maitlyn's body.

Zak moved to the other table, dropped his robe and stretched out across the padded surface as his masseur covered his nakedness from view. Lying head to head, both could easily lift their eyes up to talk to the other.

For the first ten minutes Maitlyn fought to regulate her breathing, allowing her body to relax beneath the therapeutic touch. No one spoke; nothing was heard but the sound of a soft symphony and the lull of the ocean water. Zak's seductive cadence broke through the quiet.

"How long were you married?" he asked, lifting his torso ever so slightly to peer over at her.

Maitlyn lifted her eyes to meet his stare. "Twelve years. Donald and I were high school sweethearts. We married the year after we graduated from Tulane."

"Was he the man who hurt you?"

She nodded. "Donald broke my heart," she said. "I loved him, and for the past few years he invested everything he had loving other women and other things. I probably could have handled it better if he hadn't made me feel like my own needs and wants were the cause of our problems."

"He was jealous of your independence and success."

"I don't know what he was. I just know that the man I loved with everything I had turned into this mean-spirited individual who did things to purposely hurt me."

"I'm sorry."

She smiled, lowering her eyes back to the floor. Silence refilled the space between them. "Has anyone ever broken your heart?" she suddenly asked.

They both looked back up at each other. Zak shrugged. "No. I've never loved anyone like that," he said.

Maitlyn gave him a slight smile. "I see you and my brother Kendrick have a lot in common."

Zak chuckled softly. "How many of you Boudreauxes are there?" he asked.

"There are nine of us. I have one older brother, Mason, then came me. Then Donovan, Katrina, Darryl, Kendrick and his twin, Kamaya, and the babies of the family, my brother Guy and last but not least, Tarah, whom you met before we departed."

"A large family must be nice. I hope to have a large family one day."

"You want children?"

He nodded. "I do. A man must have sons to carry on his name, right?"

"Or daughters."

He shrugged. "Or daughters. I think when you start to take it for granted, children teach you to appreciate life."

Maitlyn smiled in agreement. "Do you have any siblings?" she asked.

Zak nodded his head. "Yes. I have a younger sister, Myriam. She lives in London."

"So where is home for you?" Maitlyn questioned.

"I was born in Morocco. In Meknes."

"Your family is Berber?"

Zak's eyebrows lifted, and he seemed surprised that she would be familiar with the term *Berber,* which identified the ethnic group indigenous to North Africa. "My father is Berber. My mother is Sudanese. They met at the university, fell in love, married and made their home back in Meknes. I have a home there, one in London, a town house in New York and, of course, my cottage in New Orleans."

Maitlyn nodded, finally understanding where he'd inherited his exotic biracial looks. "Where did you go to school?"

"I graduated from Oxford, then earned my doctorate at Harvard."

"In what program?"

"Romance languages and literatures."

"Interesting! What languages do you speak?"

"French, Italian, Portuguese, Arabic and a Berber dialect."

"I'm impressed. And you play poker professionally."

Zak chuckled. "I'll retire one day and maybe go into teaching."

"I think you'd be a distraction in the classroom," Maitlyn said with a hearty laugh.

"Why do you say that?"

"Your students wouldn't be able to focus," she teased.

He smiled. "It's nice to see you laugh," he said. "You have a beautiful laugh."

Maitlyn bit down against her bottom lip, a faint blush coloring her cheeks. "Thank you! It's nice to feel so comfortable."

He nodded as he laid his head back down. "A good massage will do that for you."

So will a good man, she thought.

After the massage, the two spent a few minutes in the steam room and then relaxed in a private hot tub. Lunch was served poolside: a smorgasbord of fresh fruits, cold cuts, breads and salads for them to choose from. The two hadn't stopped talking, and Maitlyn found herself completely enamored with every word that came out of Zak's mouth.

She was only somewhat surprised to learn that he'd been raised in a strict Islamic household. There was a bad-boy edge to his spirit; his dashing demeanor and willingness to take risks contradicted that side of his conservative personality. Maitlyn was suddenly concerned about being too forward, fearful that she might do or say something that he would find off-putting. The concern must have registered on her face.

"Is something wrong?" Zak asked as he lifted a forkful of pasta salad to his mouth.

Maitlyn's eyes widened. "No. I was just…it…it's nothing," she finally stammered.

He shook his head as he wiped a cloth napkin over his lips. "No. You don't get to do that. Something's on your mind. So, please, share."

She took a deep breath as she tossed him a look. "It really isn't anything. I was just…well…I was just hoping that you didn't think too badly of me. I've been nothing but trouble for you since we sailed off."

His mouth lifted easily. "Did I say you were trouble?"

"No, but I'm encroaching on your space and—"

"And I'm enjoying your company. I think you worry too much. Let's just enjoy our time together and stop worrying. Didn't you come on this cruise to relax and have a good time?"

She nodded. "Yes."

"Then let me help you do that. I promise you'll have a good time."

"I guess I'm not used to letting someone else be in control. I've always had to man the reins. I'm a bit of a control freak, so it just feels unnatural to give that up to someone else."

"What is it you do actually?"

"I'm a *fixer* for lack of a better word. Client management, damage control, contract negotiations. You name it, I do it. If I can't handle it by myself, I'll pull together and manage a team who can."

"Your brother said you were his go-to girl when he needed something."

"My family is how I found my way into this business. I act as my brother Guy's agent. He's an actor. I try to keep Kendrick on the straight and narrow, but I'm sure you know how hard that can be. And when I get back I'll be acting as a wedding planner for my brother Darryl. I'm keeping my fingers crossed that things don't blow up between now and then."

"Well, if they do, they'll just have to wait until you return. This is your time."

Maitlyn smiled.

* * *

For almost five hours straight there wasn't much the two didn't share about themselves. Zak enjoyed their conversation, discovering much about the woman that he liked and admired. Enjoying his time with Maitlyn had kept his mind off his own issues and for a brief moment he wasn't sure if that was a good or bad thing.

Back in his cabin the two were suddenly uncomfortable with each other. Sexual tension raged like a firestorm between them. Neither was willing to acknowledge it. Both did everything fathomable to deter themselves from doing something they might regret. Zak kept reminding himself that Maitlyn was the sister of a good friend and when the trip was over, although they'd both be going in separate directions, there was the possibility they might cross paths again. It would have been a different story if she had been a stranger, someone he'd likely never see again. He sensed that Maitlyn was thinking the very same thing.

"I think I'm going to take a nap before dinner," he said, his eyes meeting hers. "We're dining with the captain tonight."

"The captain!"

Zak nodded. "He's an old friend."

"I should probably get my things and head back to my own cabin," she said. "So you can rest in your own bed." Her body swayed nervously back and forth on her heels.

Zak stared at her for a brief moment. "Is that what you really want to do?" he asked.

She hesitated for a quick second before responding. "No," she finally answered. "Not really."

"Then you stay. Besides, I like having you here."

He moved to the bar and poured himself a drink.

Scotch quickly filled a heavy-bottomed glass. When he turned back toward her, she was watching him intently. His manhood hardened with a vengeance as he met her gaze. He took a deep breath and held it in.

Maitlyn eased her way slowly to his side. Pressing her palms against his chest, she eased up on her toes and pressed her lips to his cheek, kissing him lightly. The gesture was warm and enticing.

"Thank you," she said, her voice a loud whisper.

Zak nodded.

Maitlyn smiled. "I think I'm going to sit out on your deck and read for a while. Go on up and get your nap."

"What are you reading?" he asked as she picked up her electronic reader and headed toward the sliding doors.

She shrugged. "Just a little summer read. A romance."

He smiled. "Enjoy."

As she moved outside, closing the sliding doors behind her, Zak stared after her. Romance was suddenly on his mind, too.

Chapter 7

Zak was dressing downstairs as Maitlyn took her bath. The nap had been just what he'd needed to regain his composure. His own shower had relieved the last fringes of desire he'd been feeling, and for the moment he felt like himself again. He knew he needed to get his mind right, and thinking about a tryst with Maitlyn wasn't going to serve him well.

He started his laptop and waited for the device to load. When he was able, he connected to the ship's Wi-Fi and logged into his email account. There was a lengthy list of messages waiting for his attention but only one that he was interested in. The response to a query he'd made had been timely, and once again he was reminded of why he kept his personal assistant on payroll. The woman mothered him more than he liked, but she was the epitome of efficient and always went above and beyond her duties to get the job done.

The day before he'd sent her a message, asking for any and all information she could get on Alexander Lloyd. He was now reading a full dossier on the man;

the specifics detailed everything from his personal finances to what he liked to eat on his hot dogs.

Zak was surprised to learn that Alexander Lloyd was COO and the only heir to Lloyd Banks, an international consortium of private investment firms. Reading through the documents, Zak discovered that there was some truth to the rumors that Lloyd Banks was on the verge of bankruptcy. Poor management was spinning them quickly toward financial ruin. Zak had met Alexander's father when the business was epic. Max Lloyd had given him some sound financial advice and intervened on his behalf with his first business acquisition, a dot-com start-up that he'd sold a few years later for a record profit. Zak knew that Max had suffered a stroke two years earlier and that the business was now in the hands of his family. He suddenly questioned where a man who was having some serious financial issues could find ten million dollars in hopes of winning a poker tournament. Something about Alexander and the whole situation didn't feel right, and before the cruise was over he planned on figuring out why.

As he was about to close the file, something else of interest caught his attention. Alexander had graduated from the University of Cambridge in the United Kingdom. If memory served him, Zak thought, so had his friends Gerard and Frank. Thinking he needed to know more about all of them, he quickly typed a message back to his assistant, forwarding a copy to a business associate who would also be interested in the information, and then shut down the computer.

Upstairs Maitlyn was lounging in a tub of warm water and oversize bubbles. The whirlpool bath was pure luxury and defied everything she would have thought about a cruise ship. She extended her right leg upward, drawing a palm full of water and suds over her thigh.

As she relaxed beneath the covers, her mind drifted to thoughts of Zak and a warm, familiar gnawing pulsed through her mound. It felt like it had been an eternity since she last felt that familiar ache throbbing so intensely for attention. She reflected on their time together, fantasizing about him bare chested, staring down at her as she lay sprawled across his bed. Her hand quickly slipped between her thighs, her fingertips teasing her sex. The desire to touch herself was stronger than she ever remembered, almost beyond resisting. Maitlyn stroked herself slowly at first, but as she fantasized about Zak, the more vigorous her touch became. Everything about the man excited her. His sensuous smile, the cadence of his voice, the gentle glide to his touch, everything. The more time she spent with him, the more she wanted to know about him. And with every minute they were together, Maitlyn couldn't stop thinking about them becoming more than just friends. At that moment, having Zak as a friend with some serious benefits would have made her one very happy woman.

Her mind drifted helplessly to thoughts of him touching her, his arms embracing her, his lips kissing her. She probed the ache in her feminine spirit, stroking herself all over before finally sliding a finger up and down her slit, marveling at the intensity of the sensation as she imagined that her hands were Zak's. She nudged her finger inside her sex and burrowed it deep into the silky wetness, shuddering at the wave of electricity that shot through her. Her natural wetness mixed with the sudsy water and her fingers grazed the swell of her clit, the nub full and tender. The feeling was irresistible, and surges of pleasure shot throughout every muscle in her body. She squeezed and nudged and rubbed herself from side to side, up and down, faster and faster. Mental images of Zak, his own body hard and wanting, became raw as she imagined the wealth of unspeakable pleasure the two could share.

In no time at all, toying with her sex sent her into convulsions; the resulting orgasm rose quickly and with an unexpected force. Her whole body twitched and hovered and surged. She bit down hard against her bottom lip to keep from crying out loud, Zak's name on the tip of her tongue.

Panting heavily, Maitlyn slid lower into the water, her chest heaving up and down as she fought to catch her breath. It felt good to have those hot embers that had consumed her cooling to nothing but smoke, the flames finally extinguished. Grateful for the relief, she reached for the bar of soap and a washcloth. With the tension released, she thought, dinner with Zak would be far easier to handle.

Dinner with the cruise ship's captain, Simon de Beers, was quite the event. Captain de Beers was charming and attentive, and it was obvious that he held Zak in very high regard. Their friendship was easy and comfortable, and Maitlyn was surprised to learn that the two had only met the previous year but had gone on to become great friends.

The trio enjoyed a meal of filet mignon and steamed lobster partnered with an arugula salad topped with pears, walnuts and Gorgonzola cheese. The chocolate mousse dessert with its fresh raspberry glaze was more than Maitlyn had imagined, but despite the dessert soothing her sweet tooth, she found herself barely satiated, still yearning for Zak. She let out a heavy sigh, and both men turned to stare at her.

"Was everything to your satisfaction, Maitlyn?" the captain asked.

She smiled brightly and nodded. "Everything was wonderful. I've been having an incredible time. You must be very proud of your ship and the crew."

Captain de Beers nodded. "I am. It has been an honor to serve on this vessel, and I look forward to many more years."

"Of course he is," Zak teased. "Simon is living the life. A different woman in every port, lavish meals three times a day and a boatload of employees at his beck and call. What more could a man ask for?"

Simon laughed. "You talk like you're breaking mortar and stone for a living, my friend. Weren't you vacationing in the Philippines last month and Punta Cana the month before? And what about this exquisite woman here with you now? Your life doesn't look so hard to me."

Zak laughed with his friend.

Maitlyn smiled as her gaze moved from one to the other. "It sounds to me like you both are a bit spoiled," she said.

"Maybe just a little," the captain admitted. "So what do you two have planned for this evening?"

Zak answered. "The second round of the tournament, of course. After that we might catch a late-night show."

"Make sure you do. There's a Cirque du Soleil performance in the main theater that you shouldn't miss, as well as a performance of the Broadway production *Chicago* in the lower theater. We have first-class entertainment on board."

"Maitlyn and I will be sure to catch both shows before the trip is over," Zak said as he stole a quick look at his wristwatch. "I hate to eat and run, my friend, but they'll be dealing the first hand in a few minutes and I'll need to be there."

Both men rose to their feet, shaking hands. "It was good to catch up with you, my friend," the captain chimed. "Perhaps we can do dinner again soon."

"As long as you're buying," Zak said, and both men chuckled.

Maitlyn had stood, as well, and moved to Zak's side. "Thank you, Simon. Dinner was wonderful," she said, extending her hand.

"It was a delight to meet you, Maitlyn. And take care with this one. I've heard he has a questionable reputation."

Maitlyn laughed. "I'll keep my eye on him," she countered, tossing a quick glance toward Zak.

Returning her smile with his own wide grin, Zak reached for her hand, entwining her fingers between his. He lifted the back of her hand to his lips and kissed it gently. The gesture took Maitlyn's breath away and reignited her flame all over again.

The second round of the poker tournament found Zak and Alexander Lloyd seated at the same table. Zak eyed the man coolly. Alexander appeared nervous, and for a quick minute Maitlyn felt sorry for him. It was a very quick moment. She was slightly taken aback when Izabella bounced into the room and right into Alexander's lap. She kissed him hard, a deep tongue connection that had everyone staring. When she finally released the grip she had on the back of his head, the man's chest pushed forward and his mood shifted from nervous to cocky. It was not a good look for any man.

Rising from his lap, she waved an eager hand at Zak. His expression remained stoic, not moved one way or the other by the girl's behavior. After he barely lifted an eyebrow to acknowledge her, she made her way to Maitlyn's side and dropped down onto the cushioned seat.

"How are you, Izabella?"

Izabella fanned her hand for the waitress's attention. "I'm positively giddy! How are you?"

Maitlyn smiled. "I'm good. What has you so happy?"

"Not what. Who! Isn't he gorgeous," she gushed, gesturing in Alexander's direction. She leaned closer to Maitlyn conspiratorially as she whispered, "And he's filthy rich. He owns banks!"

Maitlyn nodded. "He's a very attractive man. But he's a little old for you—don't you think?"

Izabella waved a hand. "He's forty-something. He could be ninety with all those banks he owns and I'd be fine with it!"

Maitlyn forced a slight laugh. She then greeted Lourdes, who had arrived with Izabella's requisite champagne in hand.

"Put this on Mr. Lloyd's account," Izabella said.

"No problem, ma'am," Lourdes responded. "I'll just need to confirm that with Mr. Lloyd."

Izabella rolled her eyes and waved a dismissive hand. "Whatever. Just do your job."

Maitlyn raised an eyebrow; the young woman's

tone struck a nerve. She took a deep breath, her gaze connecting with Lourdes's. She mouthed an apology. Lourdes smiled and shrugged as she moved quickly to the gaming table before the first card was dealt. Both Maitlyn and Izabella watched as Lourdes leaned in to whisper in Alexander's ear, gesturing in their direction. Izabella got to her feet and waved excitedly. Alexander strained to smile, then dropped his gaze down to the table. He mumbled something, and Lourdes's own smile dimmed dramatically. She nodded her head, acknowledging her orders. As Lourdes backed away from the table, Zak gestured for the woman's attention. There was no missing his comment, and Maitlyn smiled after reading his lips. Also, there was no missing the cold look Alexander Lloyd shot him. From Izabella's expression, it was clear that she had understood the exchange, as well.

Minutes later Lourdes returned with a refill on Maitlyn's coffee and another glass of champagne for Izabella.

"What did he say?" Izabella suddenly demanded.

"Excuse me, ma'am?" Lourdes's expression was blank.

"You heard me. Mr. Lloyd. What did he say about my charges going on his account?"

Lourdes hesitated, shooting a quick look in Maitlyn's direction. She smiled brightly. "Everything is taken care of, ma'am. Your charges are all covered."

"That's not what I asked you," Izabella persisted.

Zak's voice chimed in from behind the woman. "He said that he wasn't going to sign for anything for you. That's what he said. And instead of him being a man and telling you himself, he expected that Lourdes would deliver the bad news so that you could continue to talk to her badly."

"She said everything is taken care of. Isn't that what you said?" Izabella questioned, her head snapping in Lourdes's direction.

"And everything is. I told her that as long as you were here with Maitlyn that she could put your charges on my account." Zak pulled a hundred-dollar bill from his wallet and passed it to Lourdes.

The woman's eyes widened and her head waved vehemently. "I can't take that, Mr. Sayed."

Zak smiled widely. "You better or I'll have to report you," he said. He gave her a wink of his eye. "You've earned it," he said, his tone soft. "The fact that you were able to hold your temper with this one," he said, gesturing toward Izabella, "speaks volumes about just how good you are." Zak pressed the money into her hand.

"Thank you, sir! Thank you so much!" Lourdes retrieved the empty glasses from the table and headed back to the bar.

Zak turned his attention toward Izabella. The look he gave her was scolding, and she threw her torso back against the cushioned chair, her arms crossed over her chest, a full pout pulling at her thin lips. His name being called from the gaming area below stalled the reprimand on his lips. He drew a quick finger across Maitlyn's profile, smiled and then turned his attention back to the game, the dealer giving the final call for all players to take their seats.

When Lourdes returned with a refill of Izabella's champagne, she waved it away. Rage painted her expression as she grabbed her purse and moved back onto her feet. "Boyfriend won't be getting any of *this* to-night!" she spat.

Maitlyn shook her head, blowing a deep sigh. "It'll be okay," she said. "You deserve much better."

Izabella nodded her agreement. "Unfortunately, the good ones all seem to be taken." She tossed a glance in Zak's direction and then bid Maitlyn a good-night.

For Maitlyn, the rest of the evening was uneventful. Any further drama was played out on the gaming tables. Maitlyn loved to watch Zak play. His poker face was pristine, not an ounce of emotion showing. Alexander was not so passive; his frustrations creased his brow and colored his cheeks a vibrant shade of red. At the final bell, Zak rose victorious, moving to the next round. And by the skin of his teeth, Alexander also became one of the twelve remaining players to move on. The two men wouldn't play again until the weekend.

Zak moved back to her side. For the first time, Maitlyn sensed that a weight had been lifted from his shoulders. It seemed to relax his stance—his whole body stood less tensely. His entire demeanor felt more buoyant and relaxed. She couldn't resist asking what had changed.

Zak laughed warmly. "I've already won," he said, his tone confident. "I can relax now."

She smiled. "Sounds good to me," she said.

He winked as he gestured for Lourdes to bring him the tab to sign. As he and Maitlyn moved in the direction of the door, the waitress thanked him again for the sizable tip he'd given her. Her smile was a mile wide, and gratitude misted her eyes. Maitlyn gave her a warm hug; Lourdes's joy fueled her own.

* * *

"So, do you want to catch that show?" Zak questioned as they strolled down the passageway.

Maitlyn shrugged her shoulders. "If you want to, we can," she answered.

Zak paused for a moment, pondering what it was he really wanted to do. He suddenly shook his head as he grabbed her hand. "No. Why don't we just take a walk," he said.

Nodding her agreement Maitlyn followed as he pulled her out to the upper deck.

There was a cool breeze blowing, and a full moon sat high in the dark sky. Hand in hand, the two took a slow stroll from one end of the massive ship to the other, fully engaged in deep conversation.

"My parents haven't supported all of my choices or my sister's. We've both defied many of their wishes for us. They'd both be much happier with us if we moved back to Meknes and followed in their very conservative footsteps."

"I can just imagine how hard that must be. I know it would break my heart if my mom and dad didn't like something I'd done. Their approval means everything to me."

"It's not like that with young people today. Like Izabella. She could care less when her father disapproves of the things she does."

Maitlyn nodded. "She'll learn. We all do eventually."

A blanket of silence fell between them as they continued their slow stroll. The night air was chilly, and Maitlyn wrapped her arms around her torso to warm herself.

"Are you cold?" Zak suddenly asked, concern ringing in his tone.

Maitlyn nodded. "Just a little."

He slid his suit jacket off and wrapped it around her shoulders. They now stood so close together that Zak could feel the pounding of Maitlyn's heart. He grinned as a rising sensation prickled below his pants. His heart began to race, as well, and in that moment he wanted her badly. Maitlyn calling his name pulled him back to the moment.

"Are you okay?" Maitlyn asked, filled with concern.

He apologized, taking a deep breath. "I'm sorry. I just…" His words stalled; he knew there was no way he could explain what he was feeling.

She smiled.

"We should go inside anyway, so that I can warm you up."

"Oh," Maitlyn said, her eyes widening.

Zak laughed. "My attempt at humor failed, I see."

She shook her head. "No, not at all, it's just…" Maitlyn suddenly laughed with him.

"So now you're laughing at me!" Zak teased.

She shook her head. "Never. I am definitely laughing *with* you, Mr. Sayed."

As he stared down at her, Zak wanted nothing more than to kiss her mouth, to feel his lips pressed tightly to hers. It took everything he had not to capture her mouth beneath his own. His comment had been just shy of crude, but he had hoped to alleviate the tension he'd felt rising between them. Standing as close as they'd been standing had hardened his lines; every muscle quivered for attention. It was becoming harder and harder for him to resist her charms. And he could see it in her eyes that Maitlyn was feeling every bit as challenged, as well.

Zak finally took a step back from her, taking in deep breaths of ocean air to calm the rising sensations. He pressed a gentle palm to the side of her face and smiled. "Let's go inside," he said, his voice dropping to whisper. "Let's get you warm."

Hours later they were sitting on the deck of the cabin, Maitlyn bundled in a sweater and blanket. Over brandy and hot chocolate, the two continued to talk, laughter abundant in their conversation. Neither Maitlyn nor Zak could remember the last time either of them had had so much fun. Realizing the time, Zak shifted forward in his seat.

"I'm keeping you up. You have to be tired."

She shook her head. "I'm wide-awake actually. It's crazy."

"I know the feeling, but we'll be docking in a few hours and I want to show you everything I love about Madeira. You'll need to be well rested."

Maitlyn laughed. "That sounds ominous!"

He chuckled with her. "It does, doesn't it?"

She stood up, moving to the glass doors. "In that case, I guess I'll head up to bed."

Zak nodded. "Sweet dreams, Maitlyn."

"Sweet dreams, Zakaria."

Thirty minutes later Maitlyn was tossing and turning, consumed with thoughts of Zak. The quick shower she'd taken had done nothing to cool the rise of heat she was feeling. For a few minutes she'd blasted herself with a spray of bitterly cold water. It had seemed appropriate to ease the heat coursing through her. The cold needles of water had stung her skin, and she was thankful to have a few minutes of solace to try and sort through the wealth of emotions consuming her.

Sitting upright in the bed, Maitlyn felt her resolve wavering. She'd pondered every option and she had more reasons why she *should* make love to Zak than she had reasons *not* to. This trip had been all about tossing her inhibitions aside and having a good time. She was trying hard to rationalize why she shouldn't do just that and nothing was working. Was she really looking for a few days of no-strings-attached, rebound sex? With more questions than answers, what kept surfacing to the top of her list was if casual sex was all that she really wanted from Zak Sayed. Or did she suddenly want more?

For a brief second she thought about calling Kendrick to ask his opinion, but she quickly changed her mind. Kendrick didn't need to know that she was thinking about sleeping with his friend. She knew that once their trip was over and she walked away from Zak, her family didn't need to ever know she and the man had history.

After rising from the bed, Maitlyn moved into the bathroom. She turned on the lights and leaned against the counter to stare at her reflection. She didn't weigh a pound more than she had when she was in her teens, but her body was now rounder, fuller, having matured nicely. Her breasts still sat upright and her stomach was washboard flat, but her legs and buttocks were her best features. Maybe she wasn't twenty-eight anymore, but at the age of thirty-five, she had far more going for herself, she thought. Donald Parks had been a damn fool to let her go. Maybe Zak Sayed wouldn't want to. She smiled. Everything seemed to shift into perspective.

Maitlyn unwrapped the scarf she had tied around her head and pulled a brush through the length of her hair. The thick strands hung past her shoulders. She lightly dusted her face with makeup and lined her eyes with eyeliner. A hint of lip gloss shimmered across her full lips. Thinking it through one last time, Maitlyn spritzed herself with perfume. Satisfied with the woman staring back her, she turned and headed down the stairs.

Chapter 8

Zak was still sitting up, wide-awake as he nursed the last of his brandy. He swirled the crystal snifter in the palm of his hand. Sleep was eluding him. His body was unable to rest as he thought about Maitlyn. There was an intense chemistry between him and the beauty in spite of their differences, or perhaps because of them. He liked that they could talk so effortlessly, falling into a gentle, teasing banter with ease. He found it easy to open himself up to her, guarding nothing. Despite his best efforts he'd become an open book, and Maitlyn seemed able to read him easily.

It was becoming increasingly difficult to temper the physical affection he had for her. It had become second nature to hold her hand and Zak knew it would take nothing at all for him to take that further. He imagined himself being able to snuggle his body against hers, to kiss her lips and caress her skin, and he couldn't help but wonder if they shared the same thoughts.

The soft patter of her footsteps across the floor upstairs caught his attention. He wondered if she was having as difficult a time as he was. Crossing his legs out in front of him, he took another sip of brandy, savoring the robust taste against his tongue. Just a few brief moments passed before he heard her footsteps moving down the stairs. He watched as she came into view; her bare feet and well-toned legs peeked from beneath a white, button-down dress shirt. *His* button-down dress shirt, and there were only two buttons keeping the garment closed around her body. Zak felt a wave of heat wash over him, and he shifted forward, his knees bending as he dropped the brandy snifter back to the coffee table.

Standing at the bottom of the stairwell, Maitlyn met his gaze. She suddenly looked nervous, her eyes wide like a deer caught in headlights.

"I couldn't sleep," she finally said. "And I heard you still up."

He nodded, still eyeing her intently. She was drop-dead gorgeous and standing there barely dressed; she took his breath away.

"I've never done this before," she said as she took a step in his direction, one hand pulling at the collar of her shirt, the other clutching the hem. "I've never thrown myself at any man, but I really like you and I think you like me and…well." She hesitated, pausing at the room's center.

Zak stood up. He eased his way slowly over to stand in front of her. His eyes skated slowly over her face. He reached out a hand and brushed a length of hair from her eye. She closed her eyes and took a deep breath before opening them again. He stared, fascinated by the sight of her.

She suddenly clutched the front of her shirt with both hands, shifting her weight from one leg to the other.

"I shouldn't have come downstairs," she rambled, her voice barely a whisper. "I don't know what I was thinking. This isn't like me."

He smiled faintly. "No, it's not, but you're doing fine." His tone was intense. He tried to catch her eye, but she looked away, as if her nerves were beginning to get the better of her. He flashed another bright smile, but she still looked apprehensive. He stepped in closer to her, and Maitlyn dropped her arms back to her sides, her hands clenched tightly together.

Zak found her sexy as hell. She'd been committed when she'd come down the stairs, but her self-assurance was melting and she was like a blushing bride, virginal and timid. She'd descended the steps with a purpose, and now she seemed unwilling or simply unable to initiate the first touch. So he did.

Zak leaned forward, placing two hands on either side of her face. Maitlyn closed her eyes again. After leaning in once and then a second time, Zak finally touched his lips to hers. Her mouth was soft and tasted like mint; it mixed with the brandy on his breath. Her response was hesitant at first and then she warmed to him. The kiss increased with fervor and Maitlyn slipped her tongue between his lips. Zak slipped an easy arm around her waist and pulled her to him, nesting her body tight to his. He met her tongue with his own and the kiss became lingering. Neither seemed able to break it. Maitlyn began to moan as her body melted into his. When she moaned a second time, she must've become aware of the sound she'd made and she pulled away, her face turning a crimson shade of red. She gasped loudly, and Zak smiled.

When she opened her mouth to speak, Zak pressed an index finger to her lips. "Relax," he whispered.

Zak could feel Maitlyn's pulse quicken. She tossed her head back as Zak traced his tongue up her neck to her ear. He gently nibbled and bit the tender flesh. Zak could hear the desire in her breathing, and then he re-captured her mouth with his own. He kissed her hard, his mouth fastened tight to her, lips sliding one over the other, tongues teasing and caressing. As Maitlyn wrapped her arms around his neck, her fingers glided through his hair.

Her kisses were phenomenal, simple at first, soft, billowy touches as skin danced on skin, then probing and passionate with tongues deep, dueling playfully as they gently suckled and nibbled on each other's lips. Her body was firm and inviting against his, and his man-hood pressed hard against the fabric of his slacks. He was engorged and yearning and he knew that it would take very little to bring him to climax.

With renewed enthusiasm Maitlyn pressed her palms against his chest and pushed him gently backward to the sofa. As Zak's calves hit the cushions, he fell back, sitting down. Maitlyn moved onto his lap, straddling his body. Her body danced against him, her pelvis grinding with a vengeance against the rod of steel that pressed hard between her thighs.

"Oh…" Maitlyn gasped as Zak slipped his hands be-neath her top. She arched her back as she felt his fingers against her skin, as his palms skated over the lines of her back. He gripped her buttocks between both palms and squeezed the firm tissue as he pulled her in; the heat from her core burned hot against his lap. She was naked beneath the shirt and her nipples stood firm and erect, hardened buttons of candy needing attention.

Zak caressed every square inch of her skin, around her back, across her abdomen, up to each breast. He rolled her nipples between his thumb and forefinger, teasing them, and her, easily. Unable to resist, he ripped the shirt open, sending the two buttons flying, and pulled the garment from her shoulders. Maitlyn gasped as he trailed a path of kisses from her mouth down her neck to her right breast and then her left, his tongue lashing one nipple and then the other. As he suckled her greedily, he slipped a hand between them, and his fingers settled between her thighs as he tapped at the entrance to her secret place. She was soaked. Moisture pooled into his palm and he thrust his middle finger deep into her core as his thumb tap-danced across her clit. Maitlyn's body arched at the sweet intrusion, her hips thrusting back and forth against his palm.

As he fingered her to her first climax, his free hand entwined in her hair and he stared into her face. He couldn't imagine her being any more beautiful than in that very moment. Her eyes were closed, her mouth slightly open. Tears dripped across her cheeks. She was stunning, and it took everything in him not to explode in his pants as her release threatened to ignite his own.

Her orgasm was intense, spasms coming one after the other. Maitlyn's entire body shook against him and she hugged him tightly, holding on for dear life. As she gasped for air, Zak held her and her spent body relaxed against his broad chest. He drew a finger across her brow, leaning in to plant a damp kiss against her forehead and then her cheek. Maitlyn smiled as she snuggled her face into his neck and then she drifted off to sleep.

* * *

When Maitlyn woke the next morning, the sun was streaming in through the sliding glass doors. She woke with a start, surprised to find herself asleep on the sofa. She was naked with the white dress shirt tossed over her nudity. Zak's body was curled around hers, spooning against her backside, one arm draped across her waist. His cheek was nestled against her neck as he snored softly. She couldn't move without waking him, so she lay still, enjoying the feel of being in his arms.

Reflecting back on their night together, Maitlyn suddenly realized that their tryst had been very one-sided. Zak had ensured her satisfaction, but she had been completely oblivious to his. Not that she was complaining, but that was not how she'd imagined their first time together. In fact, she was thoroughly disappointed that she'd left him hanging. As she reflected back on every moment and each kiss and touch, Zak roused behind her, though he made no attempt at all to move.

"Good morning," he mumbled sleepily, nuzzling at her neck with the tip of his nose. He found her hand and laced his fingers through hers. "How'd you sleep?"

"Like a baby, apparently. I don't know what happened to me."

He pressed a kiss to the back of her neck, and she could feel him smile against her skin. "You were relaxed and then you fell asleep," he said. "That's what happened."

"What about you? I didn't leave you relaxed."

Zak chuckled softly. "No, you didn't. In fact," he said as he moved his other hand across her abdomen toward her breast, caressing her gently, "you left me wanting more."

Maitlyn felt her breath quickening. Zak kissed her shoulder. "We should get moving," he said. "We're docked and there's a lot to see before we have to be back on the ship."

Zak twisted himself around and sat up. He still wore the clothes he'd had on the day before. Maitlyn was suddenly embarrassed, and she pulled the shirt up over herself. It had been a very long while since she'd been naked in front of a man, and she had forgotten how awkward that first time could be.

Zak shook his head, seeming to read her mind. "Don't do that," he chastised.

"Do what?"

"Don't ever hide yourself from me," he said. He grabbed his shirt and threw it on the floor. He cupped his hand beneath her chin and lifted her eyes to his. "You are beautiful, and when you're with me I don't ever want you to doubt that. Okay?"

There was a pregnant pause before Maitlyn nodded her head. Zak leaned forward and kissed her lips. "Why don't you go up and shower. I need to check my email, and then I'll join you."

Taking a deep breath, Maitlyn nodded one last time and then eased her body off the sofa. As she moved to head up the stairs, Zak slapped her butt cheek. Her eyes widened as she tossed him a look over her shoulder. He grinned and winked at her. Shaking her head, she had to laugh.

The water felt good against her skin. Maitlyn tilted her face into the warm spray and closed her eyes. There was something happening to her, and she couldn't put it into words. Zak had her feeling some kind of way.

The man had her full and undivided attention. She liked everything about him and she loved how he took control of every situation. Her ex-husband had never taken control of anything, always expecting Maitlyn to take the lead in their relationship. When she had, he'd opted not to follow.

Maitlyn loved that Zak was all male and had no problems making sure everyone else knew it. He was confident and imposing, always taking the lead in every situation. She couldn't stop herself from wondering what it might be like to be in a relationship with a man as powerful and as dominating as Zak. To be in a relationship where she wasn't always expected to fix whatever was broken and dictate the course of their daily lives would be a welcomed change. It would be nice to be by a man's side and not a step ahead of him.

Maitlyn shook the thoughts from her mind. She had no business imagining what it might be like to be in a relationship with Zak Sayed. They barely knew each other. This was just a vacation fling that would leave them with fond memories years down the road. Nothing about her and him was supposed to be forever. She'd known that when she'd walked down those stairs last night, and she had no business thinking differently now. Maybe it hadn't been a good idea to cross the line with Zak, she mused.

Her thoughts were interrupted by a knock on the bathroom door. Zak opened it and peeked his head around. "May I come join you?" he asked.

After swiping the water from her eyes with her hand, Maitlyn peered past the shower curtain. A smile pulled at her lips. "What's taking you so long?" she said as she crooked her index finger, beckoning him to her.

Zak was naked as he moved into the room, having dropped his clothes at the door. Maitlyn's eyes widened with appreciation. The man was magnificent. Every inch of his anatomy was solid steel and the protrusion between his legs was lengthy, heavy and rock hard. Maitlyn suddenly broke out into a sweat as heat raged through her body. Her nipples hardened and the pulsing in her feminine spirit throbbed deep in her pelvis. Her knees were quivering, her whole body convulsing with anticipation, and she had to brace her hand against the wall to keep from falling.

Zak stepped into the shower with her, reaching out his hand to take hers. He wrapped an arm around her waist and slowly pulled her body to his as he spun himself beneath the water and let the warm spray wet his skin. He held them both there for a good while, allowing his body to relax beneath the moisture.

She was grateful for his arms; his hold on her steadied the quiver in her knees. He stared into her eyes, the gaze so deep that it ran shivers through Maitlyn's soul. He caressed her face, his fingers tracing her profile, before he leaned forward and softly kissed her lips. Maitlyn smiled. The sweetness of his touch took her breath away.

He trailed his hands easily up her stomach and over her breasts until he reached the curvature of her neck. Then he kissed her again, his tongue gently toying with hers. "You feel good," Zak whispered, his hands gliding back over her shoulders, across her abdomen and down between her thighs.

"So do you," Maitlyn replied, grinding her body against the length of his manhood. She pressed her cheek to his chest as she wrapped her arms tightly around his waist.

Zak suddenly grabbed her by the shoulders and pushed her against the wall. He was gentle but forceful, his intentions clear. She reached up and linked her hands behind his neck, lifting her mouth to meet his. His kiss was fierce and determined, and Maitlyn responded hungrily. His body pressed tightly against hers as she drew her hands down the length of his bare back.

"I want you badly," Zak whispered as they broke apart for air.

He dropped his mouth to her neck, and she purred as he planted delicate kisses from one ear to the other. He nibbled at her earlobe, his breath warm and his hands dancing with ease across her body. Maitlyn felt as if she were about to explode from the intense sensations his touch was eliciting from her.

Zak grabbed one hand and then the other and pulled both of her arms above her head. He captured her wrists with one of his hands, pressing them tight to the tiled wall. Maitlyn gasped when he parted her legs with the other hand and his fingertips teased her delicate folds.

Zak suddenly stepped away from her, leaving her cold. Her chest moved up and down as she panted heavily. He stepped out of the shower to the marble counter, searching his toiletry bag. A second later he returned with a condom, tearing the package with his teeth. Maitlyn watched as he sheathed himself quickly. He moved back against her, his mouth dropping to hers. He kissed her deeply, his tongue dancing with hers, his breath melting with her breath.

Maitlyn wrapped her arms around his neck and lifted one leg, easing it high against his side. Zak lifted the other, wrapping her around his waist as he held her against the heated tile. He supported her with one hand and used the other to press his organ against the door to her treasures. His desire was urgent, and with one swift stroke he entered her swiftly and easily, Maitlyn's inner lining welcoming him inside. She gasped, her nails grazing the flesh along his back, and he hesitated briefly, allowing her a brief moment to adjust to him filling her. His mouth latched back on to her mouth and he nibbled on her bottom lip before doing a two-step with her tongue.

He eased himself in and out of her slowly, over and over again. His breathing became labored and both gasped for air. He stroked her harder and deeper, the push and pull coming faster and faster. Each thrust drew him closer and closer to her, and Maitlyn clung to him.

Zak inhaled deeply and gasped loudly as Maitlyn plunged her tongue into his ear. His breathing became more rapid and short as he stroked her harder and harder. Her entire center was hot, and she craved more and more of him, unable to get enough. She felt weak as the sensations swept through her, thrashing every ounce of her energy. Maitlyn could feel Zak's sweat shower down on her, as he tried to plunge his entire body into her center.

The explosion was intense. Maitlyn's came first, her whole body erupting as her orgasm ripped through her. Every muscle quivered and her inner walls pulsed intensely around his hardness, milking him with a vengeance. Zak grunted, then groaned and when his own body exploded deep in her core, he cried out loudly.

After dropping to the shower floor, Zak leaned his back against the wall. Maitlyn was still connected against his lap. Both were weak, and he prompted her body to relax against his and guided his arms around her torso as he held her gently. Above them the shower had begun to cool and she welcomed the spray of water that helped alleviate the heat. Zak pushed her hair from her face, gently caressing her cheek as they sat embracing each other.

Zak lifted her chin and kissed her mouth one more time. She smiled sweetly as his kisses moved to her cheek and forehead. Maitlyn's eyes suddenly welled with tears. Zak then kissed each drop away, and she reveled in the intense sentiment that consumed her.

Chapter 9

Rising out of the Atlantic Ocean, Madeira seemed to be reaching for the sun. It was a dramatic volcanic amphitheater with a backdrop of natural mountains. Known as the "floating garden" island, Madeira's climate was semitropical and the island was a landscape covered in exotic wild flowers—roses and bougainvillea cascaded down in magnificent color.

The cruise ship was berthed along the breakwater. From the moment Maitlyn and Zak stepped off the gangway, she would have sworn that they'd been dropped right into heaven. It was one of the most stunning places she had ever visited. Her excitement shone on her face, and Zak seemed mesmerized by her enthusiasm.

"I felt the very same way the first time I visited. It's become one of my favorite vacation spots," he said.

Maitlyn's smile was bright, her eyes wide. "How often do you get to vacation here?" she asked.

Zak shrugged his broad shoulders. "Four, maybe five, times a year."

Her gaze narrowed ever so slightly. "You are definitely spoiled," she said.

Zak laughed. "Maybe. But today I plan to spoil you," he said. He extended his hand and took hers. "Shall we?"

She nodded as Zak waved down a taxi. Once they were settled inside, he gave the driver instructions, directing him toward the edge of town. Maitlyn was in awe as he pointed out the sights along the way, completely overwhelmed by the island's sheer beauty.

Minutes later they pulled up in front of Reid's Palace, a 126-year-old sprawling pink marvel. Situated on ten acres of lush cliff side, the hotel and its views of the Atlantic were absolutely stunning. Zak paid the driver and led her inside. The staff greeted him as if he visited every day.

"Mr. Sayed, welcome back!" the hotel concierge chimed. "How are you, sir?"

"Very well, Charles. How are you?"

The elderly man nodded. "I'm well, thank you for asking. Will you be staying with us, Mr. Sayed?"

"Not this time, Charles. I'm cruising on the *Coastal Galaxy* this visit."

The old man nodded his gray head, his smile polite and his blue eyes welcoming.

Zak gestured in her direction. "Charles, this is Ms. Boudreaux, a very good friend of mine. I'm showing her the island, and I couldn't visit and not bring her for afternoon tea."

Charles smiled, and he and Maitlyn locked eyes. "Welcome, miss."

"It's a pleasure to meet you, Mr. Charles."

Zak pressed a palm to her lower back, and they fol-

lowed Charles to the terrace restaurant. They settled
down in two wicker armchairs. In the distance they
could see the cruise ship sitting against the horizon.
Maitlyn felt herself instantly relax as she took in the
view. Minutes later she was enjoying a light meal of
English tea, freshly baked scones and finger sand-
wiches.

After reaching for the porcelain teapot, she refilled
Zak's cup. "So, tell me, when you visit Madeira, what
do you do here?"

"Nothing but relax. I get to catch up on my reading here."

"You read?"

Zak chuckled. "Why does that surprise you?"

Maitlyn laughed, realizing how the question must
have sounded. "That's not what I meant. You know
what I meant," she said.

He laughed heartily. "I hope I do," he said.

"So what do you *like* to read?" she asked, rephras-
ing her question.

"The classics mostly. I'm a big fan of Jane Austen,
Mark Twain, Walt Whitman, Anne Brontë and a few
others."

"I'm impressed. You have a background in literature,
you're multilingual and you're a card shark."

Zak raised an eyebrow. "I'm a man of many talents."

"Yes, you are. I bet you also ride horses English-
style. You collect fine art—originals only. You play
polo and you fence," she said. "Am I right?"

"No fencing. My weapons of choice are firearms. I
am very proficient with a revolver and I've shot com-
petitively a time or two."

"You are quite the renaissance man, Mr. Sayed." Her tone was low and seductive, her smile sweet.

He leaned forward, resting his forearms on the table. "My turn," he said.

She sat back, crossing her arms over her chest. "Give it your best shot."

"Your favorite flowers are yellow roses. You're obsessed with beautiful shoes. You are unreasonably competitive, and you secretly wish you could drive a race car."

Maitlyn laughed. "Three out of four's not bad."

"Three out of four! Which one did I miss?"

"I'm never unreasonable about anything," she said.

Zak's smile was wide as he shook his head. He leaned across the table and pressed his mouth to hers. The kiss was easy, much like the breeze that blew through the space. She was surprised but pleasantly pleased by his very public display of affection.

Zak studied her momentarily. "I am thoroughly enjoying my time with you, Ms. Boudreaux."

"Me, too," she said as he kissed her a second time.

After their last bite of the island's renowned Madeira cake, Zak walked her to the front of the hotel, then arranged for a private car to take them to the ferry.

"Where are we going?" Maitlyn asked as the passenger boat glided across the waters.

"Porto Santo. To walk the beach," Zak said as he draped an arm around her shoulders. He pulled her close, and she relaxed comfortably against him.

The conversation was easy as they rode the ferry to Porto Santo, making small talk about the sights and sounds around them. Maitlyn was pleasantly surprised by the stretch of sandy beach that was popular with the people of Madeira yet virtually undiscovered by tourists. The water, warmed by Gulf Stream currents and the mild weather, was a jewel, and Maitlyn quickly understood why Zak was drawn to it.

Kicking off her sandals, Maitlyn rushed to the sand's edge and dipped her toes beneath the warm ocean water. Zak moved behind her, kicking off his own shoes and socks. Maitlyn twirled in the salty spray, her sundress swirling back and forth around her knees.

She turned to face him. "It's warm!" she exclaimed, reaching down to flick a handful of water in his direction.

Zak laughed. "I know," he said as he flicked water back at her.

She giggled like a little girl as she danced around him with complete abandon.

Zak reached for her and spun her around by the waist. Her laugh was melodic and sweet. She wrapped her hands around the back of his neck and kissed him, hugging him warmly. After lowering her back to the ocean floor, he entwined her fingers with his and they strolled easily along the shoreline.

"They say the sands have healing properties," he said.

"Really?"

He nodded. "It's supposed to cure a host of ailments. Sometimes you'll see people buried in it up to their necks."

"Do you believe that?"

"I believe that this place is so relaxing that you can't help but be benefited by it."

They were easily a quarter of a mile away when they

stopped and dropped down to the fine grains of sand, staring out toward the rock formations and the water. The silence between them was golden as they sat together simply listening to each other breathe. Maitlyn swore she could even hear his heartbeat, and the pulsation was in perfect sync with her own.

He lifted her hand to his lips and kissed the back of her fingers. Heat wafted easily off his flesh. The strong scent of his cologne teased her nostrils. There was a sense of pure masculinity to it, and it suited him perfectly.

He pressed his face into her hair. He kissed the side of her head and let his tongue trace the line of her ear, pulling her earlobe between his lips. She hummed softly.

"Mmm, that's nice," she murmured.

"If I could, I would make love to you right here," he whispered loudly against her ear.

Maitlyn held her breath; the thought of them being together sent a chill down her spine.

Zak continued, "And the minute we get back to the room I plan to taste you." He trailed his hand from her knee to her upper thigh.

She inhaled swiftly, nerve endings firing beneath his touch. She wasn't accustomed to a man being so direct, and it unnerved her.

He wrapped his arms around her and pulled her to him, kissing her mouth, his tongue dancing past her lips. When he let her go, tears misted her eyes.

"What's wrong?" he questioned, his own eyes filled with concern.

Maitlyn shook her head. "It's nothing. I just…" She hesitated.

"Talk to me," Zak commanded.

"I just don't want you to be disappointed with me."

"Why would I be disappointed?"

"I don't have your experience," she answered.

Zak eyed her curiously. "I don't know if I understand."

She took a deep inhale, savoring the scent of the salt air. "You've been with a lot of women."

He smiled slightly. "I wouldn't say that."

"You're a beautiful man, Zak Sayed. Intelligent, sexy, charming. Supermodels fall out of their clothes for you."

He shrugged, not saying a word as she continued.

"I'm thirty-five years old and I've only been with one other man my whole life."

"Your husband?"

She nodded. "He was my first and my only lover. Until you."

Zak nodded. "Well, let's hope I'm your last," he said, meeting the look she was giving him.

The comment took her by surprise. "What do you mean?" she asked.

He paused, taking a deep breath as he appeared to contemplate her question. Anxiety settled in the pit of her stomach as Maitlyn waited for him to answer.

There was an air of conviction in his voice when he finally spoke. "Enjoy what's happening with us, Maitlyn. I know that I am. We have today. Tomorrow is not promised to us. And today, you have my heart. There is nothing I won't do for you. I will protect you and care for you and in this very moment you are mine and no one else's. You make me happy, and I hope to give that back to you."

They locked eyes and Maitlyn felt herself falling

head over heels into the stare he was giving her. Everything in his eyes was promising her something she had only ever imagined having. Maitlyn suddenly realized that she could never let that go and she would never expect any less from any man.

"What about tomorrow?" she asked, nervously biting down against her bottom lip.

Zak smiled. "I'll still be here. I hope you will."

Maitlyn realized that Zak had not been kidding about what he planned to do to her when they got back to the ship. The door was barely closed behind them before he pulled her into his arms. He caressed the corner of her lips with his thumb, and as he leaned in to kiss her, she parted her lips in anticipation. The minute their mouths touched, an electric current of sexual energy rippled through them.

Maitlyn was completely overwhelmed as heat and tension rose in her midsection. Zak's words were still churning in her head; she wanted to believe everything he'd said. The intensity of what she was feeling had her head spinning with desire. She wanted to be touched, to feel him inside her, to revel in the depth of emotion she knew was growing out of control between them.

Zak kissed her lips, her cheeks, her eyelids. He sucked her lower lip and then traced it with his tongue, making her softly moan. He pulled back and studied her face, and her cheeks flushed.

"I'm going to make love to you all night," he said.

She smiled sweetly. "All night?"

"Until the sun comes up," he replied.

He took her by the hand and led her upstairs to the bedroom. As they stepped into the space, Maitlyn was

taken by surprise and her eyes widened. Yellow roses
filled a multitude of containers. They sat on the dresser
and the nightstands, huge bouquets of budding blos-
soms. The sweet scent filled the room.

She tossed him a quick look as she dropped her nose
into a bouquet and inhaled the soft aroma. "They're
beautiful. When'd you do this?"

"That's my secret."

Maitlyn moved back into his arms. She was completely overwhelmed by the emotions coursing through
her spirit, knowing that Zak would never take her any
place she didn't want to go. His attentiveness and gen-
erosity made her feel special, and she hadn't felt that
special in a very long time. Outside, the wind moaned,
a soft love song blowing through the late-night air.

Zak moved to the king-size bed and sat down on the
edge. He gestured for her to come to him. Her heart
thudded and her insides simmered with tremendous
passion as she moved between his parted thighs.

Zak muttered his appreciation against her skin. Pulling her close he buried his face into her abdomen. Her
expression was adoring, her breathing heavy as she
fell against him, surrendering all of herself to him. He
pressed his lips against a spot beneath her chin. Maitlyn
arched her neck, her breath catching in her throat. He
caressed her jawline with his tongue, trailing a damp
path to her mouth. He kissed her and Maitlyn went weak
in his arms, panting softly, her eyes closed as she gave
in to the sensations sweeping through her. He pulled
her down against his lap.

"Sweet, sweet, Maitlyn," he cooed softly. "Do you
know how beautiful you are? Do you know much I
want you?"

She moaned softly. She started to speak, but Zak put his fingers over her lips. "Ssshhh!" He ran his lips up to her ear and she arched her neck back farther. "Don't talk. Just feel."

"Oh, Zak," Maitlyn whimpered. The sensations washing over her body were unlike anything she'd ever felt before. His touch felt warm and safe. She struggled to say something, anything; words seemed foreign. "Love me," she finally murmured. "Please. Love me."

Zak swung her easily onto the bed and laid her against the mattress. She sprawled, giving herself to the beautiful man. He hovered above her, easing his mouth over hers, kissing her sweetly. Their tongues came together as he explored the warm crevice, moving slowly as he did a slow waltz toward the back of her throat. He licked her lips, one and then the other, before pushing back into the warmth of her delicate mouth. She loved how he tasted against her tongue, his breath like honey, decadent and sweet.

He eased the straps of her sundress from her shoulders, sliding the garment off over her arms. Lifting her, he pulled the dress down her torso and off her body until she lay naked beside him. He moved his mouth back to hers, and the kisses grew urgent as Zak ran his palms up and down her sides. He stroked her tummy, where the soft skin pulled taut. His easy caresses made her sigh with pleasure. He kissed her longer, the touch wetter and their tongues bolder. He growled softly, moaning his desire past her lips, into her open mouth. Her insides were seething, her body yearning for more.

Maitlyn watched as his hands finally touched her, palming her soft mounds. She gasped as his touch spun heat through her. Her nipples were swollen and sensitive, desperate for his attention. He cupped the fullness of her breasts, massaged them, thumbed and tugged at the nipples until they were hard pearls between his fingertips. Maitlyn gasped loudly, her back arching.

Zak smiled. He then trailed a path across her torso with his fingers, his lips and tongue following his touch. Maitlyn squirmed, whimpering softly in anticipation. When Zak took her nipple into his mouth, sucking it eagerly, she cried out; his name rolled off her tongue in a sweet mantra. He suckled until the nipple was sensitive to the touch and then he moved on to the other.

Maitlyn twisted her hands in his hair, holding his mouth against her. Her entire body was churning inside, seething with heat. She was on sensory overload. Zak's slow and methodic loving was unlike anything she'd ever experienced before. Their first time had been about a much needed release for the both of them. This time was something different.

Zak was still focused on her breasts, nibbling and tugging on the buds, swirling the nipples between his lips and teeth. He let one and then the other snap past his lips, his tongue swirling them against the roof of his mouth. Nothing had ever prepared Maitlyn for the intense sensations. It was ecstasy beyond description. She moaned, and her body contracted as she twisted his hair around her fingers.

Her first orgasm surprised her; sharp and intense, the first crack in a rupturing dam. But there was no release; her arousal continued to build instead. She was excited beyond belief as Zak's steady ministrations took her to new heights.

He then kissed his way down her stomach, tasting every inch of her sweet flesh. He dipped his tongue into the well of her belly button, teasing her sensibilities. Maitlyn lifted her torso to watch as he continued his journey down her body. Zak eased his hands between her legs, allowing his palm to gently graze the cusp of her sex. She inhaled swiftly, holding her breath in anticipation.

He blew warm breath against the curl of pubic hair. She was suddenly anxious for his touch, lifting her pelvis with urgency. But Zak would not be rushed. He pressed his index finger against her clit and held it there, sending a bolt of electricity through her pelvis.

She cried out, "Please, baby!"

He pushed her legs open wide. Her clit was swollen and throbbing and open and wet. His fingers danced across the folds; his feathery touch caused her to thrust her body upward. He leaned in and kissed her inner thigh, nibbling at the heated flesh.

Maitlyn bit her lip as Zak made himself comfortable between her legs. His body reclined against the mattress as he brushed his cheeks against one thigh and then the other. He bent both her legs up, fully exposing the throbbing folds of her sex.

Maitlyn wriggled urgently, panting and quivering. He teased her with his fingers first, using his thumbs to open her like a present. He drew the pads of his index fingers across the folds, gently massaging the creases. She felt the tip of his tongue as he finally leaned in and tasted her. Maitlyn gasped, air catching deep in her chest. She lifted her hips and Zak buried his face deep between her legs. He lapped at her juices, probed her with his tongue. He nipped and sucked the pulsing swell into his mouth. He bathed her in saliva, his tongue flicking back and forth, hard and fast, over her pleasure spot.

Maitlyn exploded, that dam erupting in intense waves of pleasure. They ripped through her pelvis, up into her torso, out into her limbs. It was powerful and consuming, and her body seized as every muscle spasmed and rippled in surging waves. She screamed, her back arching, her hands gripping the bed sheets. Her toes curled as she writhed and sobbed, and Zak continued to lap at her juices.

As her body crashed against the mattress, Zak reached across the nightstand for a condom and quickly eased the prophylactic over the concrete rod between his legs. After moving back between her legs, he pushed her thighs open and plunged himself into her. He was like a madman as he humped against her body, frantically pushing and pulling himself inside her. It was hot and rough as his orgasm boiled to the surface, spilling out as Maitlyn met him stroke for stroke. Their frantic dance fed his pulsating release.

Dropping against her, perspiration painted his brow and his chest heaved as he gasped for air. He gathered her in his arms, cradling her close. Returning the embrace, Maitlyn pressed her lips to a spot beneath his chin, relishing the heavy rush of his breathing. They were both spent, and it felt good to just languish in his arms.

"Are you okay?" Zak whispered.

Maitlyn nodded. "Better than okay. How about you?"

Zak tightened the grip he had on her, hugging her

closer. "I love you," he murmured as he let himself drift away, snoring softly against her ear.

Maitlyn closed her eyes and exhaled, his comment spinning her into the sweetest of dreams.

Chapter 10

When Maitlyn woke the next morning, Zak was no-where to be found. The cabin was quiet, almost too quiet, and Maitlyn was slightly unnerved. After rising from the bed, she moved to the top of the stairwell and called out his name. When she didn't get a response, she let out a deep sigh, wondering where he might have gone off to.

She moved into the bathroom and eased herself into the shower. Every square inch of her body was ten-der. Zak had been right about making love to her all night long. She'd lost count of the number of times he'd brought her to orgasm. She'd woken twice to him kiss-ing her intimately, his mouth and tongue bringing her to eruption. He'd taken her from behind once, her on her hands and knees as he'd kneeled against her but-tocks. Then there had been that moment when she'd ridden him, her body straddled above his. The sun had just begun to rise over the horizon when the last quivers of passion had shaken through them both; their love-making had taken them from the bed to the patio to the living room and back to the shower. Now it hurt her to even think about touching herself.

The shower was exhilarating, and the pulse of hot water slowly revived her muscles. As she thought about Zak, she remembered his words before he'd fallen to sleep. He had said that he loved her. The sentiment had been endearing and had carried her right into her own sweet dream. She wished it was that simple, that a man like Zak Sayed could love her so easily in such a short span of time. But like he'd pointed out, enjoying what they shared today was one thing; tomorrow was a whole other animal.

Thirty minutes later she was dressed, her makeup and hair meticulous. Zak still had not returned to the room, and Maitlyn was famished. She made her way down to the breakfast buffet, eager to enjoy at least one cup of coffee before the ship was scheduled to dock at the next port.

As she checked the schedule, Maitlyn was excited to see they would be porting in Barcelona for the next two days. She had been to Spain before, and she knew that Barcelona was a beautiful city, full of everything European cities were known for. She was anxious to revisit the outdoor markets, the restaurants and her favorite designer shops. If there was an opportunity, she hoped to visit a museum or two and to photograph the architecture of the ancient churches and some of the art nouveau buildings. She hoped to do those things with Zak but didn't want to presume that he would want to do them with her.

She couldn't help but think about how quickly their time at sea was passing. More than once she'd lost track of time, a few days shifting into full weeks. They'd built comfortable routines with each other and each day allowed them to discover something new about the other. They'd taken advantage of the plans her family had made for her, each excursion and adventure a sheer joy as they did them together. There was rock climbing, cooking classes and more spa treatments. They'd also done sightseeing and walking tours. She didn't want to think about their time ever ending. A smile pulled at her mouth, joy shimmering in her eyes.

The elevator she was riding came to a halt. When the doors opened, Alexander Lloyd was standing on the other side. They're meeting was abrupt; the two practically knocked each other down: he was eager to get in and she was just as anxious to get out.

"Alexander, good morning!" Maitlyn said, surprised by the encounter.

He nodded, tossing an anxious glance over his shoulder. "Ms. Boudreaux, how are you?"

"Very well, thank you. Are you enjoying your cruise?"

His head bobbed against his shoulders and she noticed that his black eye was less black-and-blue. "I am," he answered. "How about you?"

"I'm having a wonderful time," she said.

There was an awkward moment of silence, as neither had anything else to say. "Well, you have a nice day," Maitlyn finally offered.

As she turned to leave, Alexander grabbed her arm just above her elbow.

Maitlyn's eyes narrowed. "What the hell?"

"I just want to warn you," he said, meeting her stare. "Sayed isn't who you think he is. You can't trust him.

That man's trouble, and you need to be careful. If you don't believe me, ask him about Debra."

After eyeing him a second longer Maitlyn snatched her arm from his grasp. "Don't you ever touch me again," she hissed between clenched teeth.

She then watched as Alexander stepped into the elevator. As the conveyor doors closed, he snapped, "I warned you!"

Maitlyn was breathing heavily, her heart racing. The exchange had unnerved her, and she hated that he'd been able to throw off her balance so easily. She took a quick glance around to see if anyone had witnessed the confrontation, but there were no other passengers in hearing range. She took a deep breath and held out her hands—both quivered ever so slightly.

After making her way into the dining space, she waited for the hostess to guide her to the table. The young woman was English with big baby-blue eyes and ice-blond hair.

She greeted Maitlyn warmly. "Good morning, miss."

"Good morning," Maitlyn answered, still trying to compose herself.

"Mr. Sayed is expecting you," she said.

Maitlyn nodded as she followed behind the girl. Zak was seated near the rear of the restaurant by the window, reviewing a host of papers. He smiled and stood as she neared the table.

"Good morning, beautiful," he said as he reached out to embrace her.

Maitlyn wrapped her arms around his neck, locking her hands behind his shoulders. She hugged him tightly, holding on as if her life depended on it, her body still shaking with a mind of its own.

"What happened?" Zak asked, sensing her distress.

Maitlyn was reluctant to release her grip and pressed her body tighter to his. Zak tightened his hold, saying nothing. She finally eased her grip and kissed his cheek before she pulled away. Her lips lingered a second longer than necessary. Zak pressed his palm to the side of her face.

Maitlyn smiled. "I'm sorry. I'm just being silly. Everything's fine. I missed you," she said.

Zak stared at her before gesturing toward the waiter to bring them both coffee.

"You look like you're working," Maitlyn said, nodding toward the papers he'd been focused on.

"Something like that," he said. He picked up the loose documents and returned them to the leather attaché that rested in the chair at his side.

Maitlyn thought that Zak might expound further, and when he didn't she couldn't help but wonder why. Alexander's words came back to her. Did she know Zak as well as she thought she did? And who was Debra? Did she have any right to know? She took a deep breath and let out a heavy sigh. Zak lifted his eyes to stare at her.

She met his questioning gaze with one of her own. "I ran into Alexander Lloyd at the elevator."

"Did he do something to you?" Zak asked, his eyes shifting to the red marks on her arm that she'd been rubbing since she'd sat down.

She shook her head, clasping both of her hands together in her lap. "He just said some things that unnerved me."

"What things?"

"About you. He said that I shouldn't trust you. That I don't know who you are."

Zak nodded slowly. "You really don't know me," he said matter-of-factly.

"He said I should ask you about Debra."

At the mention of the woman's name, Zak bristled. To someone who had never spent time with him, it would've gone unnoticed. But Maitlyn noticed. In fact, she felt his entire demeanor shift, and something did not feel right. She suddenly realized that she knew him better than either of them thought.

She reached out and dropped her palm against the back of his hand, her fingers gently caressing his warm skin. "I know we've only just met and we're just really getting to know each other. But—" she paused, taking a deep breath before she continued "—but I trust you. And I trust that if there was something I needed to know that you would tell me. Anything else is none of my business," she said.

Before Zak could respond, the waiter appeared at his elbow, two mugs of hot coffee in hand.

"Are you ready to order breakfast, sir?" he asked. "Or will you be partaking of the buffet this morning?"

The diversion was appreciated, and Maitlyn showed it in the wide smile that filled her face. "I really want pancakes," she exclaimed. "I want a short and maple syrup. With a side order of bacon and a glass of orange juice. I'm famished!"

Zak nodded. "That actually sounds good," he said. "I'll have the same, without the bacon."

The waiter nodded. "Very good. I'll put that order right in for you," he said as he lifted the menus from the table and walked away.

Once the man was out of earshot, Zak turned to look her at her. There was an awkward moment of quiet.

Maitlyn smiled, biting down against her bottom lip. It bothered her that there was tension between them, and she said so.

"Please don't be upset."

He shook his head. "I'm not. I'm sorry that Alexander upset you. He obviously hasn't learned his lesson."

"Forget him. He is so not worth our time and energy." She smiled brightly. "So, what are your plans today?" she asked, changing the subject.

"We should be docking in the next hour. I didn't know if there was something special you wanted to do while in Barcelona."

"I just want to spend the day with you," she said.

Zak smiled. "That's what I want, too," he said.

Zak seemed very familiar with Barcelona, and the minute the ship was docked and the captain gave them permission to debark, he guided Maitlyn downtown. Their first stop was Purificación Garcia, renowned for its Savile Row tailoring of men's wear. Their designs were sleek and sophisticated, and the staff knew Zak by name and were excited to be seeing him again. The young woman who greeted them at the door seemed particularly excited, rushing to give him a warm embrace as she kissed one of his cheeks and then the other. She seemed surprised to see him there with a woman, and she gave Maitlyn the once-over, an obvious up-and-down appraisal, before she spoke.

"Hello! My name is Ana."

"It's nice to meet you, Ana," Maitlyn said, smiling politely.

Zak chuckled under his breath. "Is Javier here?" he asked.

She nodded. "In his office. I'll call him for you," she

said as she moved back behind the counter and reached for the telephone.

Seconds later a robust man, balding at the crown, bounded up the stairs. He rushed to shake Zak's hand. "Sayed, my friend, it's good to see you," he exclaimed excitedly.

Zak smiled as the man pumped his hand up and down. "Javier! You look well."

The man shook his bulging belly between both hands. "The wife feeds me well and makes love to me a few times a week. How can I complain?"

Zak laughed. "You can't. How *is* Adriana?"

"Beautiful as always," he chimed. He tossed a look over Zak's shoulder, and his gaze met Maitlyn's curious stare. "But who is this exquisite creature?" he questioned. He pushed past Zak and extended his hand to her.

"Buenos días!" he said as he kissed the back of her hand.

Zak laughed. "Maitlyn Boudreaux, Javier Amador. Javier, this is my very special friend, Maitlyn."

"It's a pleasure to meet you, pretty lady," Javier said, still holding Maitlyn's hand tightly. "My friend has finally settled down, I hope?" He looked from her to Zak.

She smiled, shrugging her shoulders slightly. "It's very nice to meet you."

Javier smiled as he winked an eye at her. "We'll work on him, then," he said. "He needs a good woman."

Zak shook his head. "He also needs new suits," he said, changing the subject.

Javier laughed. "We can do that, too. I have some beautiful silks from a new Spanish designer that you will love. Classic designs with a very youthful edge.

Come look," he said as he gestured for the two of them to follow him.

As they made their way toward the menswear section, the women's leather section caught Maitlyn's eye. She grinned at Zak, who must've noticed the glint of excitement in her eye. "I'm going to take a peek."

Zak nodded. "Don't miss the shoes," he said teasingly.

"I wasn't planning on it," she said.

As she turned, Zak called her name.

"Yes, dear?" She turned back to look at him.

He reached into the breast pocket of his suit jacket and pulled out his leather billfold. He extracted a credit card and handed it to her. "Whatever you want," he said.

Maitlyn looked from it to him and back. It was on the tip of her tongue to argue, but something in the look he was giving her stopped her.

He moved toward her and kissed her mouth, his tongue teasing her briefly. "Whatever you want," he repeated as he turned, moving behind his friend Javier.

Ana was watching as Maitlyn stood staring at the American Express Black Card in her hand. "He's a very special man, Zak Sayed," Ana said.

Maitlyn met the woman's gaze. She nodded. "Yes," she replied, "*very* special."

She tucked the credit card into her pocket and moved into the other space. No man had ever given her his credit card to use for her own personal purchases. Her ex-husband had not been that generous. Maitlyn had never known what it might be like to have a man want to take care of her, to ensure she had pretty things on a whim, or even help pay her bills. By the time they'd been able to walk and talk her parents had taught her and her sisters to depend on themselves and only themselves for anything and everything. It had been sacrilege for them to even fantasize about any man swooping into their lives to take care of them.

Maitlyn had a pocketful of her own credit cards and the means to pay them. She owned property, had a successful business, was well traveled and the balance on her bank account was six figures high. She had always been self-sufficient and independent. Her ex-husband had hated that about her. She ran her fingers around the edge of the credit card in her pocket and shook her head.

Minutes later she was trying on shoes. Beautiful leather heels that were fueling her serious shoe obsession. She stood up in a pair of butter-soft, white leather, spiked-heel pumps and walked across the marble floor. The fit was perfect—they felt wonderful on her feet. They looked good, too, and Zak told her so.

"I like those," he said as he came into the room and took a seat. He extended his arms across the back of the chair he was sitting in and crossed his legs. "I like those very much. Pedro Garcia?"

She strolled back in front of him. "You know your designers! I'm impressed again."

"I know beautiful things on a beautiful woman."

Maitlyn giggled. "You silver-tongued devil you! Keep talking like that and a girl might fall in love," she said. She dropped her eye to admire the shoes on her feet, extending one and then the other out in front of her. When she looked back up, Zak was staring at her. She smiled, lifting an eyebrow curiously. "What?"

"Is that all it will take for you to fall in love?" he asked.

They locked eyes, and Maitlyn found his intense look

intriguing. Her heart was racing, the pit of her stomach doing flips. She reveled in the sensations for a quick minute. "Throw that in with everything else you've done since I met you, Mr. Sayed, and a girl won't be able to stop herself from falling in love with you," she answered, her voice a loud whisper.

Zak smiled and extended his hand toward her. Maitlyn took it, and he pulled her down against his lap. He wrapped one arm around her waist and his other hand cupped her chin. He stared into her eyes for a brief second, and then he kissed her, his lips dancing easily over hers. Wrapping her arms around his neck, Maitlyn kissed him back, her body melting against his.

Javier cleared his throat as he entered the room, interrupting the moment. "Passion!" he exclaimed. "It is a beautiful thing. You two have great passion."

Zak rubbed her back, his large hand skirting easily from side to side. He winked an eye at her when she noticed the rise of nature that had grown beneath her buttocks. Zak shifted, and his hard-on moved against her backside. She simply giggled.

Zak laughed, turning his attention back to his friend. "Javier, I see that Maitlyn has picked out five pairs of shoes. If you would deliver them and my suits to the ship, it would be greatly appreciated."

"Not a problem, my friend. And that other thing, too?"

"No," Zak said. He tapped the breast pocket of his suit. "I'll carry that with me."

Javier nodded. "Smart man. And if I may, I would recommend Can Gaig for dinner. It's very romantic and the *perdiz asada* is the best in the country," he said as he puckered his lips and kissed his fingers in the air.

"The food is *muy delicioso!* I can make arrangements for you."

Maitlyn looked from one to the other. "*Perdiz asada* is…?"

Zak smiled. "Roast partridge."

"Oh," she said, giving him a look. "Interesting."

"Are you ready?" he asked.

She nodded. "Oh," she exclaimed as a light bulb moment washed over her expression. "Your credit card." She reached into her pocket, pulled his card into her palm and extended it back to him.

Zak shook his head. "Put it in your purse. You might need it before the cruise is over."

She shook her head. "Really, Zakaria, I can't—" she started.

He hindered her comment with a tongue-entwined kiss. When he released her, she was panting, completely taken aback. "Keep the card, Maitlyn. Humor me. I want to spoil you. So let me."

When they locked eyes, Maitlyn nodded her head.

Zak smiled. "Whenever you're ready," he said.

Maitlyn kicked off the high heels, and Ana quickly moved into the space to take them from her hands. The girl placed them back into the box as Maitlyn stood up and slipped back into her own shoes.

"I really don't need them all," Maitlyn said as she watched the young woman carry her favorites to the counter.

Zak shrugged. "Maybe you don't. But you like them and I want you to have everything you desire."

"Zak, really—"

He held up his index finger, stalling her protests for the second time. Zak moved in front of her and kissed her lips. He then looked toward Javier, who was clapping his hands excitedly. "Handle those dinner reservations for me. Seven o'clock will be good," he commanded.

They strolled the Barcelona streets, hand in hand, from store to store, and Zak acted as her personal tour guide. It was a leisurely walk. The duo just enjoyed their time together, and the conversation was easy. Zak was attentive, funny, and Maitlyn was having the best time. She pointed her camera at him, focused the lens and snapped a picture. Zak shook his head and held up a hand in front of his face.

"You're going to break your camera if you keep doing that!"

She laughed. "You just don't like to have your picture taken."

"No, I don't."

"Well, you should. You're too pretty not to be on the cover of every magazine in the world."

Zak laughed. "Pretty? Really?"

"Handsomely so," she said, her smile bright.

He wrapped an arm around her shoulder and hugged her warmly as they continued their walk. He pointed at a large cathedral at the end of the block. "That beautiful building there is the Basílica de la Sagrada Família. It was the inspiration of a Catalan bookseller by the name of Josep Maria Bocabella. After a visit to Italy in 1872, he returned to Barcelona with the intention of building a church inspired by the Vatican."

"It's stunning," Maitlyn exclaimed.

"Wait till you see the inside," Zak said.

"Is it open?"

"When there is no mass scheduled, they sell tour tickets to help with the building expenses."

"I imagine it takes much money to maintain."

"It's taking much money to finish. They anticipate that total construction will be completed near 2026."

"And they started construction in 1872?"

"They actually broke ground in 1882. Then the Spanish Civil War stalled them for a few years when a good portion of it was destroyed."

Maitlyn tried to recall her history lessons. "The Spanish Civil War was in 1936, right?"

Zak nodded. "Beautiful and intelligent."

They walked the exterior of the extraordinary structure as Zak continued to regale her with its history. Maitlyn found the art nouveau architecture fascinating. The structure had three facades: the Nativity, the Passion and the Glory, each ornately carved, the work having been completed by hand. Maitlyn declared the Passion facade her favorite. It was especially striking for its spare, gaunt, tormented characters, including the emaciated figures of Christ being scourged at the pillar and Christ nailed to the cross. The Glory facade was still under construction and represented one's ascension to God. Zak pointed to where there would be scenes of hell, purgatory and the elements of the seven deadly sins and the seven heavenly virtues.

She smiled. "It's huge!" she said, focusing her camera skyward to capture the spire.

"It was never built to be a cathedral. It was only supposed to be cathedral-sized," he explained.

She turned her eyes to look at him. "Who's the sitting bishop?" she asked.

Her question took him by surprise. "You're Catholic?"

She nodded. "Yes."

"The basilica is under the leadership of Archbishop Lluís Martínez Sistach."

As they approached the doors to the basilica, Zak hesitated. Maitlyn didn't miss the look of alarm that crossed his face just before he pulled open the entrance and gestured for her to enter. As they stepped through the doors, Maitlyn's eyes widened in awe.

The interior was even more spectacular than the outside. They eased their way inside, and a church employee gestured for them to go on through. There was no mistaking that the young man recognized Zak; he disappeared as they headed toward the sanctuary. As they approached the pews, Maitlyn dropped to one knee. With her right hand, she crossed herself, touching her forehead, the middle of her chest, her left shoulder and then her right. She whispered a quiet "amen" before rising and taking a seat on a rear bench.

Minutes later a collared priest hurried to Zak's side to eagerly shake his hand. He kissed one of Zak's cheeks and then the other, and the two men conversed fluently in Spanish. Maitlyn stood politely with her hands clasped nervously together in front of her skirt, her ankles crossed where she sat. For a brief moment their conversation seemed intense, and concern was obvious in the priest's tone. Zak seemed remorseful, his eyes downcast, his entire stance defeated. Nothing about his demeanor resembled the man she'd come to know, and it frightened her.

Zak suddenly pressed a hand to the back of her elbow as he introduced her. His voice was low and even. "Father, this is my friend Maitlyn Boudreaux. Maitlyn, I'd like you to meet Father Bernardo."

Father Bernardo shook her hand warmly, tilting his head in greeting. "Welcome to Barcelona," he said in heavily accented English.

"Thank you, Father," Maitlyn replied.

Father Bernardo spoke in Spanish again, directing his comments at Zak.

Zak smiled as he translated. "Father Bernardo says you are very beautiful."

Maitlyn smiled. "*Gracias,* Father!"

The elderly man nodded. He spoke again, and Zak responded in his native tongue.

Zak laughed. "He also asked me when I planned to make an honest woman out of you."

Her eyes widened. "What did you tell him?"

"I told him that if I have my way, then you will be my wife when we return next year."

"Zak!" Her stunned expression made both men laugh.

Father Bernardo spoke again, his hands moving excitedly.

Zak narrowed his eyes. "Father Bernardo said that he will pray for God to fulfill my wish."

Maitlyn was still stunned by the exchange; the surprise shown plainly on her face. The two men spoke briefly one last time; then Father Bernardo reached for her hands and took them both between his own. He tilted his head, his smile warm.

"Safe travels, my child," he said.

"Thank you, Father."

She and Zak watched as he hurried away. When he was out of sight, Maitlyn sat back down and Zak dropped to the pew beside her. She had a host of questions and not a clue where she should begin.

Minutes passed before she finally spoke. "How long have you known Father Bernardo?"

"It's been over ten years now. I met him through a friend. I was having a crisis of faith and she thought he might be of some assistance to me."

"Was he?"

Zak tossed her a quick look. "He helped me put my doubts into perspective."

"Interesting."

"Not really."

Silence billowed between them a second time. Zak's low tone broke through the quiet.

"Alexander told you to ask me about Debra. Well, Debra was my fiancée."

Maitlyn's eyes widened at the mention of the woman's name. "Your fiancée?"

Zak nodded. "Debra's family was from Madrid. She and I met at Oxford. She was a chemist and she specialized in cancer research. She was hoping to discover the chemical compound that would eliminate the disease forever. We were young and we were in love."

"What happened to her? Why didn't you marry?"

"The week before our wedding, she was murdered by a man who had a vendetta against me. There are people I've done business with who are a little unsavory. He was not happy about our transaction, and he took it out on her. The lust for money and power will make some men do things the rest of us live to regret."

Tears misted Maitlyn's eyes. "Zakaria, I am so sorry. But you can't blame yourself for something someone else did."

Zak met her stare. "I don't."

She took a breath. "What happened to the man that killed her?"

Zak paused for a minute before responding. "I killed him."

Chapter 11

Zak stared down at Maitlyn, who was sleeping soundly. He realized he could have stared at her forever. She was the most enchanting creature to ever bless his life. There was something about her spirit that had moved him exponentially. Pulled him from a very dark space into an amazingly hopeful abode. He liked where he was and knew, beyond any doubt, that he would do anything and everything to stay as long as Maitlyn was there by his side.

He pulled the sheets up and over her naked body, then eased his own down the stairs. He paused at the bar and poured himself a shot of Scotch before moving out onto the deck and dropping down into the chaise lounge. He took the first sip of his drink and leaned back, his legs crossed in front of him. There was a sliver of moon in the midnight sky and a cool breeze blowing off the water. Zak inhaled deeply in an attempt to relax, wanting to will his body to sleep.

Earlier in the day he'd been afraid that he had scared Maitlyn off. Sharing the details of his history had not been easy, something he'd bottled and stored away ages ago. Visiting the cathedral where he and Debra had planned to marry had been a turning point for him. Walking through that door with Maitlyn had moved that hurt from his heart; his memories of Debra and their time together were no longer a source of pain. For the first time since forever he was at peace, his memories a warm reminder that opening his heart to a woman could be a good thing. He took a second sip of his drink, then placed the tumbler onto the glass-topped table at his side.

He had sworn to never fall in love again. He couldn't imagine being vulnerable with any other woman, being protective of her, needing her, wanting her. But Maitlyn had managed to get under his skin and peel away every protective wall he'd put into place in a very short amount of time. She had made him comfortable from day one. Her own vulnerabilities had been written all over her, and she hadn't been afraid to show them. He'd seen the hurt on her face and all he had wanted was to wipe it away. He never wanted to see that pain in her eyes again. Whether she realized it yet or not, he loved the woman with an emotion so deep and so hard that he couldn't begin to imagine her not being in his life.

Initially he'd struggled because of his relationship with her brother. He had great respect for Kendrick and what Maitlyn didn't know was that Zak had her brother to thank for helping him after Debra's death. But because Kendrick knew his past, he'd been concerned about what his friend would think about him and Maitlyn pursuing a relationship. It was important to him that Kendrick supported them both. He had wanted to call, to get his friend's approval, but that hadn't been an option.

In spite of not being able to get her brother's blessing, Zak had been excited about getting to know her better, to see just how compatible they really were together. Not once had he considered that he might be a rebound from her previous relationship. And even as the thought crossed his mind now, his instincts told him otherwise. He reached for his drink and tossed the last of it back, and the bitterness burned the back of his throat.

Something about Alexander Lloyd was still not sitting well with him. How he'd even known about him and Debra concerned him. Why he'd thrown Debra's name in Maitlyn's face infuriated him. Alexander needed to be dealt with. But he needed to figure out what the man was up to first. He took a deep breath, his mind racing. The glass doors sliding open interrupted his thoughts.

"Hey," Maitlyn said as she stepped out onto the deck. "Couldn't you sleep?"

He shook his head. "I didn't want to wake you," he said.

"You could have," she said as she moved to his side.

His eyes rolled over her naked body, admiring her form shadowed against the darkness. He reached out his hand and guided her onto his lap. Maitlyn straddled his body, pressing her pelvis tight against his flaccid member. His skin was hot, as if he were on fire. The intensity of it ignited every one of his nerve endings, and he felt like he might combust. He was grateful for the cool breeze that suddenly washed over him.

Zak's hands skated across her back, lingering against her backside. He held her close as she nuzzled her mouth against his neck, leaving a trail of kisses against his skin. He lightly pressed his mouth to hers and let the tip of his tongue trace her lips. She tasted sweet, and he felt as if he were addicted, desperate to have her. He slipped his tongue inside her mouth, delicately exploring the warm cavity. After a minute of soft, sensual kissing, he coaxed her tongue past his lips and gently sucked on it, bringing an immediate reaction from her beautiful body. Her breathing increased, and she moaned as she pulled away and looked into his eyes. The stare he gave her back was dreamy and lust-filled.

He rested his hand on the inside of her bare leg as the other stroked her neck gently, pulling her face back to his. She parted her lips in invitation, and they kissed again. Maitlyn whimpered, her arousal swelling thick and full, rising to meet his.

Their loving was easy and slow. He was buried deep in the center of her core before he realized it. Maitlyn rode him easily. It was a gentle back-and-forth, up-and-down gyration that synced sweetly with the natural push and pull of his body. Together they rocked with the side-to-side lull of the ship as the ocean breeze rained a salty spray against their naked bodies. He held her tight, and she hugged him close. And when the sheer beauty of their loving exploded, the clouds above parted and a sliver of moon smiled down on them.

Zak watched Maitlyn as she consumed her second lobster. Her love for food was abundant and her appetite was voracious. Her enthusiasm at mealtimes was engaging. He smiled widely.

"How do you eat so much food and not gain a pound?" Zak asked. "I've never known a woman who enjoys food as much as you do."

Maitlyn laughed. "I do like food, and thankfully I

have a very high metabolism. If I didn't eat, I'd be insanely thin."

"Well, we can't have that. I love your curves."

Maitlyn smiled brightly. "That's good because I don't need you teasing me when I order dessert."

"And what sweets are you eating tonight?"

"I'm torn between the butterscotch cheesecake and that chocolate mousse raspberry cake thing. Oh, Oh, Oh!" she exclaimed. "Why don't I order one and you order the other?" Maitlyn proposed.

Zak shook his head. "I was planning to order the carrot cake."

"Well, you can order the carrot cake *and* the cheesecake. If you do it, they won't raise an eye."

He laughed. "Oh, so you want to make it look like I'm the greedy one!"

"Yes!" She laughed with him.

He shook his head and gestured for the waiter.

"Yes, sir?"

"Ms. Boudreaux and I will share one of every dessert on tonight's menu, please."

"All of them, sir?"

Zak's head nodded up and down. "Yes."

"Right away, Mr. Sayed."

"Thank you."

"All of them?"

He shrugged. "I would only do that for you, my darling," he said.

"I don't think you know just how much you have done for me," Maitlyn said, meeting the look he was giving her. "I was a real mess when I boarded. You've renewed my spirit more than you realize. I feel like myself again, and I have you to thank for that."

Zak reached for her hand and squeezed it. "Do you believe in fate, Maitlyn?"

"I do," she said with an easy nod.

"Well, I think fate put us here together, and I think it's destiny that our paths have crossed when we were both in need."

"I like that," she said.

They laughed over dessert, sharing each decadent plate. When they were down to one piece of pecan rum pie, there was a struggle for it. Their two forks dueled like swords.

Maitlyn giggled loudly as Zak hesitated just long enough for her to swoop in for the victory. She slid the last piece of caramel, nuts and crust into her mouth and smacked her lips.

"No fair," Zak proclaimed.

"Stick to cards, Mr. Sayed. You can't win in a dessert battle," she teased.

He dropped his fork on the table and leaned back in his seat. "I'm stuffed. I don't know how I'm going to play tonight."

"You've got this game won, remember?"

Zak nodded. "I remember."

"Did you change your mind about that?"

"Not at all. I just don't know how I'm going to play *comfortably* tonight. I've overeaten."

"We could go back to the room and work it off," Maitlyn mused as she sucked her index finger into her mouth and withdrew it slowly.

Zak chuckled. "We could, if I had a few extra hours. Unfortunately, my darling, I have to head to the casino."

She snapped her fingers. "Oh, well. Can't blame a girl for trying!"

Zak hesitated, staring at her.

She lifted her eyebrows, curiosity painting her expression. "What are you thinking about?" she asked.

"We will dock in Morocco in the morning. I am going into Meknes to see my family. I want you to go with me. I want to introduce you to my mother."

Maitlyn's expression went blank. Her gaze locked with his. "Your mother?"

He nodded. "Yes. I think you should meet my family, Maitlyn."

Maitlyn pulled a hand to her heart and patted her chest. "I don't know why that suddenly made me nervous," she said, fanning her face.

His eyes narrowed. "I think you do. So, tell me."

She leaned back in her seat and took a deep breath before she spoke. "What's happening between us, Zak?"

"What do you want to have happen?" He crossed his hands together atop the table.

They continued to hold the stare they shared. Her voice dropped to a loud whisper.

"The time we've spent together has been magical. It's like a dream come true. But I haven't forgotten that this cruise is going to come to an end, and you're going to go your way and I'm going to go mine."

"Is that what you want, to go your own way?"

"No," Maitlyn said, conviction ringing in her tone. "I don't want that. I don't want that at all."

"So why does meeting my mother make you nervous?"

"Because it's your *mother*."

"Yes, it is. And I want my mother to know the woman I'm in love with. I want her to meet the woman who will be my wife and bear my children. We can come back to

Morocco at any time for that to happen, but we're here now, so there is no reason for us to put it off."

A tear rolled down Maitlyn's cheek. "Do you really love me?"

Zak chuckled. "Haven't I told you?"

"You were half-asleep, Zak. We'd just made love. I didn't think—"

He waved a finger at her. "I *never* say anything I don't mean. Ever. You should know that by now, Maitlyn."

"I know, but all this is happening so fast, Zak. I know I have feelings for you and I…well…I don't…" Her eyes flitted back and forth anxiously.

"So you don't love me?"

"No…yes…I mean…I do…I don't know.… I…" Tears suddenly filled her eyes as she looked at him.

"It's fine," he said softly. "Clearly, you and I need to talk more. But for now—" Zak stood up and cast a quick glance down to his wristwatch "—I'm late. The next round will be starting soon. We can finish this later." Zak pressed an easy kiss to her cheek, then pulled his suit jacked closed around his torso. He headed for the exit.

As he reached the door, Maitlyn called after him, a sense of urgency in her tone. She hurried behind him, coming to a halt at his side.

"Yes?"

She pressed her palms against his chest, tilting her head to stare at him. "I do love you," she said emphatically. "I love you, but I'm scared. I've never been so scared."

Zak nodded as he pressed his hand to the side of

her face. "Trust me. Trust this! But more importantly, trust yourself."

She nodded her head. "I can't wait to meet your mother," she whispered.

Zak nodded his head and smiled. He leaned down and kissed her lightly on her damp lashes, the tip of her nose and finally her full lips, savoring the sensation as they trembled beneath his own. His eyes were closed, his lips lingering, the kiss long, tender and expressive. When he finally drew back, there was a tear in his eye.

Zak's game face was fully engaged, not an ounce of emotion emoted from him. Everyone within earshot whispered about him being so calm and collected, almost cold in his demeanor. Only Maitlyn knew otherwise; electricity spun with a vengeance between them. More than once he met her nervous stare, holding the gaze, and when he did, the intensity of his stare made her head spin and her body suddenly break out into a cold sweat from the heat.

She did love him, Maitlyn realized. It seemed unfathomable to her to care so much about a man she'd known for only a few weeks. But with Zak, everything about the two of them together felt right. There was still so much she needed to discover about him and even more about herself that she wanted to share. Envisioning the sheer magnitude of the relationship that they could have together excited her. She could easily envision spending the rest of her life in Zak Sayed's arms.

The four winning players moving on to the finals of the poker tournament each stood to thunderous applause. There was Lucille Talley, a professional poker player who hailed from France; Dr. Prentiss Manning, a psychologist from Chicago; Alexander Lloyd; and Zakaria. Zak had won his last hand with two deuces, in a nail-biting turn that had everyone sitting on the edge of their seats until that last card had been turned.

He had observed a wide grin filling Maitlyn's face as she clapped proudly. Uncomfortable with the attention, Zak eased himself away from the group, moving to the viewer's box where she sat. He gestured for Lourdes, who was instantly at his elbow to take his order.

"Yes, sir, Mr. Sayed?"

"Lourdes, coffee, please."

"Yes, sir, Mr. Sayed. Black, sir?"

Zak nodded, and Lourdes hurried away. She returned almost immediately with a fresh cup for him and a refill for Maitlyn. "Will that be all, sir?"

"Yes, thank you," Zak responded. He tossed Maitlyn a look. "Do you want anything, darling?"

"I'm good, thank you," Maitlyn answered.

Lourdes extended her congratulations, then moved on to fill someone else's order.

"You had me scared," Maitlyn said, the excitement still shimmering in her voice.

Zak smiled. "Did you doubt me?"

"You called his bid, raised it and you only had a pair of twos in your hand. I had all the confidence in the world in you," she said facetiously.

Zak laughed. "I told you to trust me. Why is that hard for you to do?"

"It's not hard. And I do trust you. But you still had me nervous, Zak Sayed!" Maitlyn said with a smile.

He nodded as he took a sip of his brew, his eyes wandering around the space. The casino was still a wealth of activity, the party just getting into full swing. From the dance floor on the other side of the room, Izabella waved both of her hands in the air. Her smile was wide as she danced against her current suitor; the man appeared completely engaged. Zak pointed her out and him, and Maitlyn laughed.

About an hour later, as they both continued to watch the crowd, enjoying the atmosphere, Maitlyn caught sight of Alexander Lloyd. The man was huddled in a corner with his two sidekicks; the three men were once again in serious conversation. She was just about to point them out to Zak when Lloyd turned and looked directly at her. Their conversation stalled and suddenly all three were staring in her direction. She reached a hand out and touched Zak's forearm just as Alexander muttered something under his breath and all three turned in opposite directions. Just like that Lloyd was gone. The moment felt a little surreal.

Zak eyed her curiously. "What is it?" he asked.

She shook her head as she forced a smile back to her face. "Tell me more about your family," she said, shifting her focus.

He smiled.

"You'll meet my parents. My mother, Dr. Grace Sayed, was born in south Sudan. She and her family took refuge in Australia to escape the civil wars. Her parents sent her to school in England, where she met my father, Hassan Sayed."

"Is your father a doctor, too?"

Zak shook his head. "No. My father is an attorney and somewhat of a legal rights activist."

"Wow! That's interesting. I look forward to meeting them."

Zak smiled, leaning forward in his seat. "I should forewarn you that I haven't seen my parents in quite some time."

"Oh? What happened?"

"They didn't support my relationship with Debra. She was Catholic. They are Muslim. They wanted me to marry a nice Muslim girl."

Maitlyn tossed up her hands. "So the first time you've seen them in a while, you bring another Catholic girl? You're a glutton for punishment, aren't you?"

"I promise you it won't be an issue."

"Maybe not for you, but your mother might not be so accommodating."

"My mother will love you."

Maitlyn rolled her eyes.

Zak smiled. "It's not as bad as it would be with my sister—trust me on that."

"What do you mean?"

"My sister left home after she refused to marry the man my parents had betrothed her to. It was quite a disgrace to the family name."

"Her marriage had been arranged?"

"When she was three. The groom was five. By the time the two hit their teens, she couldn't stand him." Zak shrugged. "That was much worse than my non-Muslim fiancée!"

Maitlyn laughed. "What have I gotten myself into?"

"I am hoping," he started as he leaned forward and kissed her lips, "that you are now on the journey of a lifetime."

She kissed him again. "I think it's going to be a wonderful ride," she said.

"I have something for you," Zak said.

She grinned. "What?"

He slipped a large hand into the breast pocket of his jacket and pulled out a flat velvet-covered box.

Her eyes widened as Zak passed the gift to her. "I picked this up for you when we were shopping in Barcelona and thought it would be beautiful on you."

Her hand shook as she lifted the lid. Inside rested the most beautiful necklace Maitlyn had ever seen. The jeweled delight shimmered against the satin lining. The circular design was platinum, encrusted with diamond baguettes interspersed with round, brilliant-cut diamonds and ten large emeralds. It was jaw-dropping.

"Zak, it's beautiful," Maitlyn exclaimed.

He nodded. "It will be beautiful on you."

"Thank you! Oh, my God, thank you!" She moved to wrap her arms around his neck, still admiring the piece behind his back. "I don't know how to thank you!"

Zak laughed. "Enjoy it. That will be thanks enough," he said.

Maitlyn tightened her grip and kissed his cheek. Her lips finally moved to his mouth. "I love you."

Zak kissed her back. "I love you, too."

Chapter 12

Zak couldn't believe how quickly the cruise was flying by. They didn't have much longer at sea and only a few more ports to visit. He and Maitlyn had been taking full advantage of all the activities offered by the cruise line and were having an incredible time together.

If Maitlyn hadn't been traveling with him he probably would not have participated in a third of the things that she had wanted to try. And Maitlyn wanted to try everything. Her enthusiasm was infectious, and her boldness excited him. She was also highly competitive, and her zealousness was intriguing. They'd participated in a cooking class, learning the nuances of handmade pasta. Then there had been the rock climbing; Maitlyn had beat him to the top. They'd been challenged in a trivia competition, missing the title by one question, and had ice-skated and also learned to use a trapeze. There'd been line dancing, dancing at nightclubs and simply dancing just because music was playing somewhere close by. Only once had Maitlyn given in and agreed to rest by the pool and do absolutely nothing at all.

Remembering the last time he'd been so happy gave

Zak pause. He had never imagined feeling this good about anything and certainly not about a woman he'd only just come to know. But something about Maitlyn had gripped his heart from the first moment, had wormed its way deep beneath his skin and was refusing to let go. The woman was overwhelmingly intoxicating and had become the sweetest addiction. As he thought about her, he couldn't help but wonder what might happen when their trip was done and it all came to an end. He knew what he wanted but didn't know if he could make that happen. As Maitlyn strolled in his direction, he couldn't help but wonder what she was thinking about.

The touching started in the elevator. Zak's lazy caresses blew like an easy breeze. He looked deep into her eyes but said nothing. If felt like an absolute eternity before either moved; the elevator door opened and closed again and again. He leaned forward and planted a firm kiss on her lips, his hands still teasing her flesh. Maitlyn instinctively wrapped her arms around his neck, and, like a chain reaction, their mouths parted slightly and Zak slipped his tongue past her lips. At the same time his hands snaked beneath her blouse and his fingers caressed her belly. She moaned at his touch.

Maitlyn pulled away from him, slipping out of the elevator into the corridor. She dragged him along behind her, and they giggled as they made their way back to Zak's cabin. Behind the closed door, Zak reclaimed her mouth as he ripped her blouse from her body. Maitlyn gasped as the silk fabric fell to the floor. He cupped both of her breasts in the palms of his hands, kneading the full tissue as his fingertips teased one nipple and

then the other, pinching the firm nubs until she was
withered from the sensations.

There was no making it to the bedroom. Zak grabbed
her hand as they sunk down against the living room
floor. He then bowed his head and took the nub of rock
candy between his lips. Maitlyn felt her body convulse
at his expert sucking and nibbling and barely noticed
his hand stroking her legs beneath her skirt as he suckled her like a baby. But she did notice when his fingers
pushed past her lace thong and the tips teased her center.

Zak was on a path of exploration as his fingers teased
her folds. She felt a finger slide slowly inside her and his
thumb circling her clit. She felt him push her legs apart
just seconds before he plunged his tongue against her.

Nothing prepared her for the sensory overload; every
single nerve in her body shuddered with joy. Her head
was light, heat flooding every square inch of her skin.
Her entire body felt like it was going to explode as she
quivered beneath him. She gasped, moaning his name
over and over again as she shook.

Zak moved up against her body as he took her into
his arms and rolled her half-naked to a rest against his
chest. His extended length pressed against her opening;
his pants opened wide beneath her. Sliding her body
down, Maitlyn pulled at his pants and he lifted his hips
as she rolled them off his body. They tangled at his feet
and he kicked them off and spread his legs beneath her.

She focused her attention on his hardness. He was
thick and smooth and his length pulsed in her hand.
Maitlyn leaned forward, and her tongue slowly circled
its head. Zak gasped loudly, sucking oxygen in hard.
She lifted her gaze to see his face, and his eyes were
closed, joy and bliss painting his expression. Taking

more of him into her mouth, her tongue swirled around as she stroked him slowly up and down. She sucked him hard and fast and when she felt him tighten, ready to explode, she stalled her ministrations. Zak sucked in air again, and his body shivered from the loss of her touch.

Maitlyn reached back into the pocket of his slacks and pulled his wallet from inside, then grabbed a condom from the pocket where he kept them hidden. Tearing at the wrapper with her teeth, she pulled the prophylactic out and pulled it around his member. When he was completely sheathed, Zak held her by the waist and slowly rolled his hips up. Maitlyn felt his width begin to stretch her open. She stared into his eyes, her mouth parted, as he entered her opening, sliding himself easily into her.

His strokes were short and slow at first, then longer and harder as she rode him more vigorously. His hands alternated between her breasts and her ass, his fingers kneading and squeezing. Up and down, over and over again she slammed her body against his, their pelvic bones tight, one against the other. She felt her orgasm rising and she bit her lip as the rush of emotion swept over her again and again. Zak's face was twisted, hinting at his own impending climax, and both screamed the other's name at the same time.

Hours later Zak turned on the shower and waited for the water to warm. By the time it was heated, Maitlyn had made her way into the room and steam had begun to paint the tiled walls. She stepped into the hot spray, and Zak followed. He reached for the bottle of liquid soap and filled his palm, drawing his hands across her body until her skin was coated with lather. She returned the favor, and they stood caressing each other sensually.

Standing behind her, Zak pressed himself against her buttocks as his hands danced across her breasts, her belly, roaming teasingly over her body. He kissed her shoulder, and then went lower, kissing down the length of her spine. When he reached her buttocks he planted sweet little kisses over each cheek.

Maitlyn's head waved from side to side, her breathing becoming heavier. Zak then gripped her hips and pulled her to him, dropping his face into her hair. She felt good in his arms, her curves against him like the missing piece to a puzzle that was his life. He gripped her tighter and moaned her name against the back of her neck. He pushed her forward, and she braced her arms against the wall as he entered her from behind. His loving was intense and urgent, the connection sweeter than anything he'd ever known. The crescendo was magnanimous and both of their orgasms erupted like a perfectly timed orchestra.

Maitlyn rolled against the mattress. As her eyes fluttered open and then closed, she thought about what might be ahead once the cruise ship ported. Zakaria had been confident about his family liking her, and his assurances eased the tension that curdled her stomach. She prayed that he was right. Her eyes were still closed as her hands reached out for Zak. She wasn't surprised to find the bed beside her empty. Zak was like a magician the way he seemed to disappear in the early morning hours. She couldn't help but wonder what was so important to him. She was discovering that Zak kept much of his business close to the vest; secrecy seemed to be a necessary evil for him to accomplish all he needed to do. But he'd promised her complete honesty, and she knew if she asked he would be straight with her. He had already forewarned her that she might not always like his answers, so Maitlyn had pretty much decided that she didn't always need to know everything.

They were making an announcement over the intercom. The cruise director called for passengers who were taking part in the shore excursions. They were docked in Rabat, and their floating hotel would be there for the next thirty-six hours. After rising from the bed, she moved into the bathroom to dress, knowing Zak was down in the dining room, ready and waiting for her.

She was dressed in a casual white pantsuit that she'd paired with a simple gray T-shirt as she made her way into the room and toward the table where Zak sat. A dark gray scarf was loosely wrapped around her neck, and her hair was pulled back into a tight braid down her back. He nodded approvingly.

Maitlyn was surprised to see him out of his requisite dark suit. Zak looked dashing in linen pants and a traditional Moroccan tunic with a banded collar. Both were the color of butter, and his top was lightly embroidered in an intricate pattern of gold-and-brown threads. She smiled sweetly as she dropped down into the seat beside him.

"Good morning," she said brightly.

Zak returned the look she was giving him. "Good morning. You were sleeping soundly when I left."

"You always steal away when I'm snoring."

He nodded. "That's true."

She giggled. "You were supposed to say that I didn't snore."

He laughed. "Except that you do snore. Loudly."

Maitlyn laughed again. "I do not!"

Zak changed the subject as he gestured for the waiter. "Are you hungry? We'll need to be moving soon. It's almost three hours by train from here to Meknes."

"I'm actually too nervous to eat," she said.

Zak smiled. "Don't be nervous. We'll have a very nice time."

"I didn't doubt that. I always have a good time with you. It's just that we're going to see your parents. That's a big thing, Zakaria."

He chuckled. "I imagine it is."

"Just wait until I take you to meet my parents. Then you'll understand what I'm talking about."

"I've already met your parents," Zak said nonchalantly.

"When did you meet my parents?" she asked with surprise.

"Kendrick introduced us last year when they came to visit him in Paris. I believe they were there for their anniversary. We all had dinner together at Chez Chartier."

Maitlyn's eyes darted back and forth. She knew her parents had spent time in Paris with her brother, but she didn't recall her mother ever mentioning that she had met any of his friends. If her mother had met Zak, she couldn't imagine Katherine not being excited to share that little bit of information with all her single daughters. Then Maitlyn remembered, she had still been married.

Zak laughed. "Your mother likes me. Your father, too, I think."

Shaking her head, Maitlyn laughed with him. If only things would be that easy for her with his folks. She drank a quick cup of coffee and ate a bowl of oatmeal and bananas. When Zak had finished his eggs and toast, they grabbed their overnight bag and headed to the train station.

Zak spoke perfect Arabic and had no problems maneuvering them through the train station to purchase tickets. They traveled in a first-class train car with two other passengers. The train meandered its way toward Meknes and his family home. As he stared out the window toward the familiar terrain, a look of homesickness flashed across his face. It was brief, just a quick hint past the many walls Zak kept in place to shield himself from others.

The countryside from Rabat to Meknes was a slow descent that took them from sea level up into the hills. Maitlyn snapped pictures as Zak fell into a state of reverie, memories clouding his thoughts. He withdrew slightly, seeming disinterested in any conversation, so she let him be and chatted instead with a lovely Asian couple vacationing from New York. The two-plus hours flew by quickly, and when the train came to a stop in Meknes both Zak and Maitlyn took deep breaths.

Meknes, known as the "Versailles of Morocco," was one of Morocco's most striking imperial cities. Home to a beautiful blend of diverse and distinct cultures, Meknes was a nice representation of a very modern Morocco.

After hailing a taxi, Zak served as her tour guide, pointing out the bustling Ville Nouvelle, the labyrinthine Medina and a host of relaxing plazas and green spaces. With its many palaces, mosques, gardens, lakes, granaries and stables, Meknes was a dream city.

He pointed to a gathering of boys tossing a Hacky Sack between them. "That was me, many, many years ago," he said. His smile was wide, the first Maitlyn had seen since they'd disembarked. It warmed her spirit, moving her to smile with him. He continued to point out all the tourist treasures until the taxi pulled up in front of a large home with meticulous landscaping.

Maitlyn's nerves shifted into overdrive, and her hands were clenched tightly in her lap. Zak dropped a hand to her knee and caressed it gently. "Relax," he said. "This is my home. We will stay here tonight. My parents live close by. We'll walk over once we get settled." He paid the taxi driver, tipping the man generously.

Maitlyn let out a sigh of relief as she followed behind him, her eyes skating across the magnificent home. Zak led her up the steps to the door of the white stone structure. It had a circular turret in front and a large bay window. A gray-haired old man threw the door open, greeting him warmly in Arabic.

Zak gestured in her direction, saying something she didn't understand. The old man nodded as he bowed repeatedly and reached for the bag in her hand. "Maitlyn, this is Solomon. Solomon takes care of the property when I'm not here. If you need anything, just let him know."

She smiled and nodded as she greeted him warmly. "It's very nice to meet you, sir."

Solomon continued to bob his head up and down.

Zak laughed. "Don't let him fool you. He understands English perfectly."

The old guy winked at her and turned, disappearing down a short length of hallway.

Maitlyn spun in place, taking in the views, as she

moved from room to room. The decor was traditional, but the amenities were clearly upscale. The home was beautiful, and she told Zak so.

"Thank you. I don't get the opportunity to visit as much as I would like."

"Maybe things can change?" Maitlyn questioned. "Maybe this a turning point for you."

He moved to her side and kissed her forehead. "Let's make it a turning point for us both since it will soon be our home."

The ringing of a telephone stalled their conversation. Solomon came rushing back into the living space to answer it. His conversation was curt and quick. After hanging up, he relayed a message to Zak.

Zak took a deep breath, annoyance creasing his brow. He met her curious gaze. "My mother is waiting for us," he said.

Solomon corrected him. "His mother, she is expecting Zakaria. Zakaria never brought a woman home before." He tossed Maitlyn a look, as if he was forewarning her.

Maitlyn nodded her head. "Thank you, Solomon." She shifted her gaze to Zak, her eyebrows raised. "She doesn't know I'm coming?"

Zak smiled, shrugging his broad shoulders.

"It's not funny!" Maitlyn exclaimed. "There is absolutely nothing funny about this, Zakaria."

Both Zak and Solomon chuckled warmly.

Maitlyn shook her head. "Why don't you point me in the direction of the restroom so I can freshen up before we *surprise* your mother," she said, her tone brusque.

Zak smiled and nodded, still chuckling as Solomon rushed to show her the way.

Minutes later the two were slowly strolling the streets, then rounding the corner toward the center of town.

Zak had gone quiet again, but this time Maitlyn wasn't having it. "Why wouldn't you call your mother to tell her we were coming?"

"It wasn't necessary." He cut an eye at her.

"Even Solomon thought it might have been necessary."

"Solomon is afraid of my mother."

"Well, that makes me feel better," Maitlyn said, her words dripping with sarcasm.

"There is nothing for you to worry about, Maitlyn. *I* am *not* afraid of my mother."

"Well, I am. In fact, I'm terrified, and I haven't met her yet."

He reached for her hand and squeezed it. Mindful of where they were, Maitlyn knew that any public displays of affection would not be looked on kindly. She squeezed back, then pulled her hand from his.

"Solomon said that you've never brought a woman home. Did your mother never meet Debra?"

He glanced at her. "She did. But I never brought Debra to Meknes. They met while we were visiting my sister in London."

"Did your mother like her? I know she wasn't happy about her religion, but did she like her at all?"

Zak sighed. He lifted his hand to acknowledge a group of elderly men who were eyeing them both curiously. When he called out in Arabic, the gathering waved excitedly, their gestures clearly welcoming him home. Just when Maitlyn was wondering if he planned to completely ignore her question, he answered.

"My mother was not happy about our relationship, but she had great respect for Debra and the work she did. Both being in the medical field gave them common ground."

Maitlyn nodded. Before she could ask anything else, he pointed her through the gates of a large property. Beyond the gates led them into a narrow alleyway and then to an old wooden door. She pointed to a sign against the gate; the text was in Arabic.

Zak translated it for her. "It says Riad Sayed, or loosely translated, Home of the Sayed Family."

Nodding, Maitlyn took a deep breath. She pulled at the gray scarf that was twisted around her neck. After unwinding it, she stretched it easily in front of her. She draped it over her head and crossed it beneath her chin, allowing the ends to fall over her shoulders and down her back. Zak stared as she adjusted her suit jacket. When she was done, she tossed him an easy smile. He pressed a hand to her cheek and leaned in to kiss her lips.

As they stepped through the door, into the center courtyard, Maitlyn stared in awe. The home was a palace, large and expansive. The courtyard was exquisite, everything in full bloom. There was an extraordinary fountain that bubbled softly with flowing water into the center of a large pool, lemon trees heavy with fruit and lush greenery that had a tropical feel. The building itself was square with two levels, and the entire upper level had a balcony that ran its circumference, overlooking the garden from all sides. It was beautiful.

"Is this where you grew up?" Maitlyn asked.

Zak nodded. "My sister and I use to play down here," he said softly.

A stern voice called to him from across the way. "Zakaria? Is that you son?"

"It is, *Ommah*. How are you?" he asked.

Maitlyn turned to stare as Zakaria's mother sauntered toward them. The woman was nearly as tall as Zak. Her skin was the color of black ice and smooth as silk. Her features were chiseled, her cheekbones high and her lips full. She wore a royal-blue kaftan exquisitely detailed with beads and embroidery, and as it billowed around her lean frame, she reminded Maitlyn of the supermodel Alek Wek walking the runway. She was beautiful. Zak had inherited his mother's eyes, the orbs deep and dark, and her cheekbones. She imagined his other features had to be from his father.

Maitlyn observed from close by as Zak's mother wrapped him in a warm embrace, hugging him to her tightly. There was no mistaking that she had missed having her only son near to her. She pulled back, still clutching him by the shoulders as she stared, her eyes taking in every one of his features as though she was memorizing each crease and dimple. She pulled him back to her.

"I have missed you, Zakaria."

Zak tilted his head ever so slightly. "I have missed you, too, *Ommah*."

She tossed a glance in Maitlyn's direction, appearing slightly taken aback by the woman's presence. "Who do we have here?" she asked, looking from Zak to her and back.

"*Ommah*, I want you to meet Maitlyn Boudreaux. Maitlyn, this is my mother, Dr. Grace Sayed."

His mother nodded, moving to stand in front of Mai-

tlyn. "Boudreaux? Are you related to Kendrick, my Zakaria's dear friend?"

Maitlyn nodded. "Yes, ma'am. Kendrick is my
brother."

"How delightful! We just adore your brother! And
what a beautiful name, Maitlyn."

Maitlyn smiled. "Thank you. It's very nice to meet
you, Dr. Sayed."

"Please, call me Grace, dear," she said as she hugged
Maitlyn easily.

Maitlyn smiled. "Thank you."

"Come sit," Dr. Sayed ordered. "I have mint tea and
almond cookies waiting for you," she said as she turned,
leading the way to a table in the corner of the garden.

Zak gestured for Maitlyn to follow behind his
mother. "Where's *Baba?*" Zak asked.

"He should be back soon. He went to the mosque for
prayer earlier. I have no doubt he is still there with the
men talking about nothing important."

Zak smiled, cutting an eye toward Maitlyn.

Dr. Sayed poured them all a cup of mint tea and then
took the seat next to her son. "So, my child, you are
home. To what do we owe the honor?"

"I wanted Maitlyn to see Meknes and to meet you
and *Baba,*" he said.

His mother looked from him to her. "She must be
special then," she said, her gaze meeting Maitlyn's.

"She is," Zak said matter-of-factly. "Maitlyn is very
important to me."

Maitlyn smiled, noting the head-to-toe look his
mother was giving her. Before his mother could respond, his father's voice boomed through the space.
"Zakaria! Son! Welcome home!"

Zak jumped to his feet, his wide smile warming his face. *"Baba!"* he exclaimed as the men threw themselves into each other's arms. "It's good to see you, *Baba.*"

Hassan Sayed kissed both his son's cheeks, then hugged him tightly a second time. Zak and his father looked more like brothers than father and son. Zak's warm complexion was only a hint darker than his father's pale caramel tone. He had his father's wavy black hair, succulent mouth and chiseled jawline.

"And this must be Maitlyn," Hassan Sayed chimed, moving to shake Maitlyn's hand and kiss both her cheeks. "My son has told me much about you. Welcome to our home."

Maitlyn tossed Zak a quick look. His mother's eyebrows were also raised, curiosity wrinkling her brow.

"Thank you for having me, Mr. Sayed. It's a pleasure to meet you."

"You are as beautiful as my son said you were."

Maitlyn blushed. "Thank you."

Dr. Sayed cleared her throat. "I guess I was not home for that conversation," she said, tossing her husband a harsh look.

Mr. Sayed laughed, waving a dismissive hand at her. "My son and I talk about things a father and his son should share. He's a man now, not a baby who tells his *ommah* his secrets."

Clearly annoyed Dr. Sayed rolled her eyes. She took a sip of her tea and reached for a cookie. "Maitlyn, you must try the almond cookies. They are Zakaria's favorite," she said.

After taking a bite of the sweet offered to her, Maitlyn savored the delicate flavor of the cookie. "Mmm! They're very good."

"How long will you be in Meknes?" his father asked.

"We leave in the morning," Zak said, explaining that they had come in on the cruise ship and that he had one more night of tournament play.

His mother waved her hand. "You need to give up that foolishness and come home. You should be settled down with children of your own by now," she chastised.

"Soon, *Ommah*," Zak said.

His father laughed warmly.

"Well, we have room here for you and we can make arrangements at the riad on the corner for Maitlyn. I do not think they have any tourists staying tonight," Dr. Sayed said.

"That won't be necessary. I had Solomon air out the house. Maitlyn and I are already settled in," Zak said.

His mother didn't respond, but her jaw tightened and her expression showed her displeasure. "I'll call and make sure Solomon airs out both bedrooms. And he should stay to chaperone. We do not want anyone to think there is anything inappropriate going on," she said.

Zak met his mother's gaze. A wry smiled pulled at his lips. "You do that, *Ommah*," he said.

Grace's smile was strained. "So, tell me, Maitlyn. How is your brother?"

"He's doing very well, ma'am. Thank you for asking."

"He was very nice, your brother. And respectful. I think he went to the mosque with Zakaria and his father, although your family is not Muslim—is that correct?"

Maitlyn took a deep breath. "No, ma'am, we are not."

She grunted.

Mr. Sayed shook his head. "We are having a feast to welcome you home," he said. "This is a good day for an old man!"

"It's a small affair," his mother said. "Family and a few friends. If I'd had more notice, I would have had a big homecoming for you." She moved to her feet. "I need to go check on the cook. Maitlyn, please make yourself at home."

"Thank you," Maitlyn said.

As she exited the room, Hassan tossed up his hands. "Your mother, she never changes. Do not let her upset you."

Zak shook his head. "She doesn't, *Baba.*"

Maitlyn liked Zak's father. The man's gregarious personality was engaging. He asked a lot of questions about her and her family and seemed genuinely interested in knowing more about her. There was no missing that Zak and his father had an incredible relationship, a solid bond and friendship. His father's approval meant a lot to him. She didn't think he felt the same about his mother. After a solid conversation, Mr. Sayed excused himself to go check on his wife and the progress in the kitchen.

Zak let out a deep sigh. "Are you okay?" he questioned.

Maitlyn appreciated his concern. She nodded her head. "I really like your father," she said.

"He likes you."

"I don't think your mother likes me."

"My mother will love you. Give her time. She just finds it difficult to deal with things she can't control."

Zak grabbed her hand. "Come with me," he said as he pulled her along and up the short flight of stairs.

"Where are we going?"

Zak smiled as he rounded the balcony to a room on the other side. He opened the door and led her inside. Maitlyn smiled back as she turned in circles, taking in the view.

His childhood room was covered in posters, a world map and the February 20, 1989, cover of the *New Yorker.* Most were badly faded, but they were still in place. A twin bed sat against one wall and there was an extensive collection of books on the built-in shelves. A child's telescope sat on the center of the desk and an old boom box rested on the nightstand.

Maitlyn clapped her hands together. "This is too precious," she said as she examined the many titles in his collection. "Oh! *Moby Dick, Treasure Island, Grimm's Fairy Tales!* You were a nerdy little boy," she exclaimed.

"I was not that nerdy," Zak said with a laugh.

She moved to the other side of the room and picked up a lined notebook that rested on the desktop. She found his childhood handwriting amusing. The printing was neat and orderly, and there was a circular rotation to his signings. She paused to read what he'd written, then lifted her eyes to his. "You wrote poetry!"

"I *tried* to write poetry," he said sheepishly.

Maitlyn started to read out loud. "Roses are red—"

Zak jumped to her side and snatched the book from her hand. "That's not necessary," he said.

Maitlyn laughed. "I think you're blushing."

"I'm not blushing," he said as he dropped the binder back on the desk. He eased an arm around her waist and drew her to him. The laughter waned beneath the warmth of his touch.

Maitlyn pressed her palms to his chest. Zak brushed his fingers along her profile, pushing her scarf off her head and back around her neck. They stared into each other's eyes. Their connection was soul deep; the link between them was all-consuming, like nothing she had ever known. Dipping his head, Zak brushed his lips over hers, barely touching the soft tissue. He dipped once and then again before finally dropping his mouth against hers and kissing her hard.

Chapter 13

A voice from the doorway interrupted the couple as they stood enjoying their quiet moment together. Both turned at the same time, suddenly feeling like they'd gotten caught with their hands in the cookie jar.

"Excuse me," the young woman staring at them said. Her arms were crossed tightly in front of her and she looked uncomfortably nervous.

"Aalijah." Zak said. The hand that had been wrapped around Maitlyn's waist dropped down to his side. "What are you doing here?"

Aalijah smiled, her gaze narrowing slightly. "Hello, Zakaria. Your mother thought you might be up here. She asked me to call you down."

Zak nodded. His expression shifted into something Maitlyn didn't recognize. He and the other woman staring at each other suddenly made her uncomfortable. She looked from one to the other as Zak suddenly remembered his manners.

"Maitlyn, this is Aalijah Dar. Aalijah is an old family friend. Aalijah, this is Maitlyn Boudreaux.

Aalijah nodded her head, tossing Maitlyn a quick

wave of her hand. "Your mother says you should come down. Your guests are arriving." She turned abruptly and disappeared from view.

Maitlyn looked up at Zak. "What was that all about?" she asked.

Zak shook his head. "We'll talk about it later. We need to go down," he said, ignoring her question.

As they made their way back to the courtyard, they noticed a small crowd had begun to gather. Zak shook his head. "So much for a small affair. She's probably invited half the town," he snapped, clearly displeased.

Maitlyn found Zak's tone disconcerting. Something had him upset and she didn't think it had anything to do with the family members who were throwing their arms around his shoulders to welcome him home. But rather everything to do with the teary-eyed young woman at his mother's side. Maitlyn stole glances toward Dr. Sayed and Aalijah, who were huddled together in the corner. Aalijah was clearly distressed, and Dr. Sayed was trying hard to console her.

Aalijah was a pretty girl with an air of innocence about her. Her head and chest were covered by a hijab, the traditional veil worn by a Muslim female beyond the age of puberty in the presence of adult males. Her crystal clear complexion was free of makeup, and she looked much younger than Maitlyn imagined she really was.

Zak's father suddenly grabbed her hands and pulled her along to meet Zak's family and their host of friends. Everyone was warm and welcoming. His aunt and cousins were in deep conversation about their planned trip to the Hawaiian Islands. As his aunt was bemoaning her fear of flying, Maitlyn stole a glance around the room. Zak had joined his mother and Aalijah. His mother was talking with her hands; her limbs waved erratically back and forth. She wasn't happy, and, judging by the expression on Zak's face, neither was he.

A soft bell chimed through the room. Zak's father gestured for his son's attention, waving him to his side. Zak turned an about-face, leaving his mother in midsentence. He paused at Maitlyn's elbow.

"I'll be back," Zak said.

"Where are you going?"

"Mosque. The men have to gather together for the afternoon prayer. We won't be long," Zakaria said.

She nodded. She had gotten comfortable with him practicing his daily prayers. They'd had many conversations about their respective religions. She knew that Zakaria had once struggled with his faith. They had even talked about her converting to Islam, and she had promised to give it serious consideration if he would do the same with Catholicism. They had discussed that with love and dedication they would find a happy medium for themselves and if not, they would agree to disagree.

After the men had gone, Dr. Sayed moved to her side. "Maitlyn! I do hope you are enjoying yourself."

Maitlyn smiled. "Yes, I am. Thank you so much for your kind hospitality."

Dr. Sayed nodded. "We will sit down to eat as soon as the men return. I'm sure you're famished."

There was a moment of awkward silence before Dr. Sayed tossed her next question at Maitlyn. "So, tell me, dear, what is the nature of your relationship with my son?"

Maitlyn's eyes widened. "Zakaria and I are very good friends and we've grown very close."

"But you both just met—is that correct?"

"Yes, ma'am. We haven't known each other long, but I care deeply for your son. I guess you can say it was love at first sight."

"You're saying you love my son?"

"Very much. And he loves me."

Dr. Sayed stared at her with an appraising gaze, her jaw tight. It was a moment before she spoke. "Zakaria has always been impetuous. There are many decisions he's made that he's come to regret."

She hesitated as though she expected Maitlyn to respond, but then she continued. "Has he told you about Debra?"

Maitlyn nodded. "Yes. He's told me everything."

Dr. Sayed's eyebrows lifted slightly. "Well, that was a disaster on many levels, and unfortunately it cost that young girl her life. But she was not a good fit for Zakaria. He needs a woman who understands him, who knows his culture and is familiar with his background."

"A girl like Aalijah?" Maitlyn blurted out.

Dr. Sayed met her stare, and the two women eyed each other as if a gauntlet had been tossed down and battle declared. She finally broke the silence. "Exactly. I see you've met Aalijah?"

"Zak introduced us briefly. I know she's an old family friend."

His mother's mouth lifted into a slight smile. She called out to Aalijah, beckoning her over.

"Yes, Mother?" Aalijah replied.

"Come sit with us, dear. I was just explaining things to Zakaria's *friend*." She spat the last word out as if it were clobber in her mouth.

Maitlyn tossed Aalijah an easy smile, but the woman didn't smile back. She suddenly became sick and tired of the attitude. She didn't have a clue what she'd done for Aalijah to be so cold toward her. Aalijah calling Dr. Sayed "Mother" also raised her eyebrow.

"Zakaria was less than forthcoming with you, Maitlyn. Aalijah is much more than just a family friend. Mr. Sayed and I have been acquainted with her parents for many years, even before our children were born. When Zakaria and Aalijah were very young, they were promised to each other. Her father and Hassan negotiated their marriage contract.

"After going to school in London, Zakaria turned from our ways and I have not been happy with some of his behavior. But, like some men, he needed to sow his wild oats and with there being so many Western women like yourself indulging that bad behavior, it was easy for him to disregard his responsibilities. After Debra's death, Zakaria realized the mistakes he'd made and had recommitted himself to Aalijah. I'm confident that the two will soon be married as Allah has willed.

"You are only a diversion, of sorts, and I'm certain that now that Zakaria is home, my son will come to his senses and fulfill his obligation. Aalijah is the only daughter-in-law his father and I will recognize," she finished. Her words stung.

Dr. Sayed looked from Maitlyn to Aalijah, then stood up. "The men should be returning shortly. I need to ensure the food is ready." She moved back toward the door into the home's kitchen.

Maitlyn lifted her eyes to look at Aalijah, who had been staring at her since Dr. Sayed's rant.

"I love him," the young woman whispered. "And it hurts me to see him with other women. But I will be a good wife. Faithful and loving. I know that soon Zakaria will only have eyes for me. You are cheap and easy, and he will not want that type of woman to bear his children."

Maitlyn shook her head slowly. She stood up, her gaze still locked with Aalijah's. "I wouldn't hold my breath waiting for him if I were you. And there's nothing cheap or easy about me. In fact, I'm a tad high maintenance, but Zak loves me anyway. And I love him. And no one, not you or his mother, can change that. You better think about asking that daddy of yours to find you another man. Zakaria is mine, and I don't plan to give him up without one hell of a fight."

From where she stood, Dr. Sayed stared, her mouth open in disbelief. Moving across the room, Maitlyn extended her goodbyes to the women of Zak's family and, with an easy wave toward Dr. Sayed, she exited the Sayed home.

Zak had been watching Maitlyn sleep, sitting on the bed beside her for over thirty minutes. He'd been staring at her, completely enamored with the woman.

After returning to his family home, he'd found his mother in a complete funk. She had been unhappy that Maitlyn had abandoned them so casually. His aunt had tattled about the exchange between the women. Everyone else had been dismayed by Grace Sayed's conduct toward her guest. Zak should not have been surprised, but he was. He'd hoped that his mother would have been on better behavior. He had nothing to say to Aalijah, having already told her before that he had no intentions of honoring the agreement between their two families. Their arranged marriage would be a figment of everyone else's imagination because he was not hav-

ing any part of it. Aalijah had always been like an an-
noying little sister, and there was nothing about her that
moved his spirit the way Maitlyn did. Both women had
been appalled by Maitlyn's response and even more dismayed when he and his father both had laughed, clearly
amused by Maitlyn's boldness.

As Maitlyn stirred, swiping sleep from her eyes, he
gently caressed her hip and side, reclining his body
against hers. He felt her stiffen beneath his touch, and
he knew that she was angry. "I'm sorry," he said softly,
his warm breath whispering against her ear.

"You should have told me that you were engaged,"
Maitlyn snapped.

He laughed. "I am not engaged. Not to Aalijah. The
marriage was arranged when I was ten years old. I had
nothing to do with it."

"Someone forgot to give your fiancée that memo."

"I think you took care of that."

A pregnant pause swelled between them. Maitlyn
took a deep breath before speaking again. "You're
mother hates me."

He shook his head. "My mother actually likes you.
She admires your strength and your—" He paused.
"What's that word?" He suddenly nodded. "Your *chutz-
pah!* No one has ever challenged her like that."

"She still wants you to marry Aalijah."

He shrugged. "She wants what's best for me. But she
still thinks I'm that ten-year-old little boy. She doesn't
know me well enough now to know what's best for me."

Maitlyn sat up, pulling her knees to her chest as she
wrapped her arms around her legs. "Am I what's best
for you, Zak?"

"Without a doubt," he said as he sat up beside her and wrapped his arms around her shoulders.

Maitlyn leaned her head against his shoulder. She closed her eyes tight as Zak held her for a good minute.

"I have a surprise for you," Zak suddenly said.

Maitlyn eyed him suspiciously. "A surprise? What kind of surprise?"

"Come see," he said as he extended his hand and pulled her from the bed.

Zak led her to the rooftop patio of his home. The midnight air was warm and welcoming. The space had been strung with white lights that shimmered against the night sky, adding to the wealth of stars that sparkled overhead. A table had been set in the center of the patio: two place settings anchored a centerpiece of pillar candles and freshly cut flowers. Maitlyn smiled as she stared out over the landscape and the lights shimmering in the distance.

"It's so pretty!" she exclaimed, her eyes widening.

Zak pressed a hand to the small of her back and leaned in to kiss her cheek. "I thought you might be hungry. Solomon made us a special dinner." He pulled out a chair for her. Once she was settled, he poured them both a cup of mint tea.

Zak prepared their plates, ladling a beef and apricot tagine into a bowl and couscous piled high with steamed vegetables onto their plates. After Maitlyn was done with her plate, Zak revealed a delicious crème brûlée with orange blossom water. With the meal finished, they sat beneath the twinkling lights, lingering over their mint tea.

"I do apologize again for my mother," Zak said.

Maitlyn shrugged. "I understand your mother. You

are her baby. If you marry a nice girl from here, the chances are more than likely that you will come back here to Meknes and she will have you around every day. My mother's not much different. She hates when her children aren't around. And now that she has grandchildren, she's even worse."

Zak nodded. "You will be like that one day."

Maitlyn laughed. "I probably will."

Zak shifted his chair to her side of the table and set it directly in front of her. He leaned forward in his seat, his elbows resting on his knees as he took her hands in his. "Do you trust that I love you?"

Maitlyn met his intense gaze. "Trusting, that is why I'm here."

He nodded. "Promise me that you won't ever let anyone, not even my mother, put any doubt in your mind about how I feel about you."

"I promise," Maitlyn said.

Zak leaned in and kissed her mouth. Still holding on to her hands, he stared up at the shimmering sky, the bright stars and twinkling lights, and he whispered a prayer of thanksgiving.

The taxi pulled up in front of Riad Sayed, and Zak asked the driver to wait. "We won't be long," he said to the man, his native language rolling off his tongue. Standing before the wooden door, Maitlyn took a deep breath and then a second, fortifying her nerves before having to face Zakaria's mother one last time. His parents were sitting in the courtyard, enjoying their morning meal, when they stepped through the entrance hand in hand.

"We came to say goodbye," Zak said, leaning down to hug his mother.

"I hope you won't stay away so long the next time, Zakaria," Dr. Sayed said. She wrapped her arms around her son's neck and hugged him tightly.

He and his father shook hands. "Thank you, *Baba*," he said.

Mr. Sayed kissed his son, hugging him tightly. "It will all be well," he said. "And I am proud of you, son."

"We will cross paths again soon, *Baba*," Zak said.

Maitlyn smiled, the tender moment between Zak and his father warming her spirit. As she watched them, Dr. Sayed caught her attention. She shifted her smile in the woman's direction.

"Thank you for welcoming me into your home, Dr. Sayed. Your hospitality was greatly appreciated."

The woman nodded. "I regret that some unpleasant things were said yesterday. I hope you'll accept my apology."

Maitlyn nodded. "I appreciate that," she responded.

Mr. Sayed wrapped his arms tightly around her, kissing one cheek and then the other. "You are welcome here always, Maitlyn," he said. *"Assalamu alaikum."*

"Wa'alaikum assalaam," she responded, wishing that peace would be with him, as well.

Dr. Sayed moved to Maitlyn's side, shaking an index finger in her direction. "You continue to surprise me," she said.

Maitlyn smiled. "I hope that's a good thing."

Dr. Sayed nodded. "It's impressive." She embraced Maitlyn warmly, leaning in to whisper into her ear. "My son is my life. Do not forget that."

Maitlyn nodded. "Never. He is my world, as well.

Chapter 14

The ship had hit bad weather, and it rocked back and forth in the choppy waters. There was a lengthy line out the door of the medical office; many passengers sought relief for the nausea that had them looking a pale shade of green.

Maitlyn stood on the top deck, peering over the rail out to the water. She was mesmerized by the heavy swell, the blue-green blanket peaked with white foam. She deeply inhaled the fresh air, a salty spray tickling her nostrils.

Zak had gone back to the room to nap. He wanted to be well rested for the final game of the tournament. After lunch he'd been quiet and withdrawn, so Maitlyn had retreated to the ship's library to read while he did his own thing alone. Things were good between them, and she was confident that after his win it would only get better.

She was startled when Alexander suddenly appeared by her side. He held his hands up as if in surrender, a wide smile filling his face. She took a step back, regarding him with suspicion.

"You scared me!" Maitlyn said, a hand pressed to the center of her chest. Her heart was racing.

"I didn't mean to," Alexander said, his smile widening. "I saw you standing here alone and wanted to take a moment to apologize for upsetting you before."

She continued to eye him warily.

"I should not have spoken out of turn about Mr. Sayed. I hope you can forgive me."

"It's fine, Mr. Lloyd. I appreciate your apology."

He nodded excitedly. "I hate that things took a turn with us. I thought we had gotten off to a good start. I was almost certain that we were going to have a good time together," he said. He drew his fingers across her arm.

Maitlyn jerked her arm away, taking a step back from him. "Please, don't touch me," she said, raising her voice.

She tossed a glance around to see who might be close. There was another man close by and a couple snuggling on the lounge chairs. On the other side, a handful of people were watching a movie on the big screen.

Alexander held up his hands a second time. "I didn't mean any disrespect," he said.

Maitlyn took a deep breath. "Alexander, again, I appreciate your apology. Maybe during another time or place things might have been different."

He turned toward the railing, clasping his hands together against the chest-high metal bar. Much like Maitlyn had just been doing, he looked down to the water below. "It's something, isn't it?"

Maitlyn cut a quick eye to where he stared, then turned back to look at him. She nodded. "It is."

"Initially I was reluctant to cruise. With all the horror stories I heard. Between that one that hit the rocks in Italy and that one that caught fire and became stranded, it all made me a little nervous."

Maitlyn didn't bother to respond as he continued.

"The stories I found most interesting were the ones where people just fell overboard and disappeared. I imagine it would be kind of hard to just fall, though," he said as he stood up on his toes and peered down. "That's not an easy thing to do. I imagine it wouldn't take much to toss someone overboard, though," he said, turning to look at her.

Maitlyn was suddenly uncomfortable, and her intuition kicked in with a vengeance. She took two steps backward. "Goodbye, Mr. Lloyd," she said, turning abruptly and rushing in the opposite direction.

Behind her she could hear him laughing. "Until the next time, Ms. Boudreaux!"

It was only after she had secured the lock on the cabin door that Maitlyn was able to breathe. The deep inhale and exhale of oxygen slowly calmed her nerves, and the anxiety she'd been feeling subsided. Something about Alexander Lloyd scared her, and Maitlyn didn't scare easily. She took another deep breath and stole a peek at her image in the entrance mirror. She didn't want Zak to know about her encounter; she didn't want anything to upset him before he had to play. She was probably just being paranoid unnecessarily, she mused. After swiping at her eyes, she pinched color into her cheeks and pulled a brush through her hair. Forcing a smile onto her face, she stared at herself one last time, praying that Zak didn't sense anything wrong.

As she climbed the stairs to the second level, she

could hear Zak snoring softly. When she reached the top of the landing, she spied him sprawled facedown against the mattress. He was buck naked, and as she tiptoed to the foot of the bed, her eyes were drawn to the curve of his backside. His bottom was like a nice-size basketball that needed to be palmed. As if he was reading her mind, he reached a hand behind his back and scratched his left cheek. Maitlyn slapped a hand over her mouth to stop herself from laughing out loud. Even as he slumbered, his presence made her instantly comfortable. She felt safe whenever she was with Zak. She stood watching him for some time, and then he rolled across the mattress and sprawled on his back.

Maitlyn undid the buttons to her slacks, pushing them and her thong down to the floor. She lifted her shirt over her head and reached around to unsnap her bra. She suddenly needed to feel him. She needed to feel her skin against his skin. She was desperate for his touch. She crawled up between Zak's legs, slowly easing her body against his. Lying on top of him, she molded her body to his, her legs sprawled open atop his, her arms resting where his arms laid. Zak instinctively wrapped his arms tightly around her.

Maitlyn snapped out of a deep sleep when Zak kissed her forehead. He smiled sweetly.

"What time is it?" she asked.

He glanced at his watch. "Almost seven. I need to head up to the casino."

She sat up quickly, throwing her legs off the side of the bed. "Why didn't you wake me? I didn't realize it's so late."

He shook his head. "It's not. I just need to be there

early. We won't start playing until sometime after nine. You have plenty of time, so don't rush. Just meet me when you're ready."

She nodded. "I will. We can celebrate your win with a late-night dinner?"

He leaned in to kiss her again. "That sounds like a plan." He headed toward the stairs, then turned back to face her. "How do I look?"

Maitlyn smiled. "You look great," she said. And he did, decked out in a Tom Ford double-breasted tuxedo. It was classic black, with matching wide-peak satin lapels and satin trimming along the cuffs. He could have easily donned the cover of *GQ* magazine.

With a wink of his eye, Zak blew her a kiss and bounded down the stairs. Happier than she could ever imagine, Maitlyn headed into the shower.

The players had been introduced to a fanfare of applause. As Zak slid into his seat, the dealer announced the beginning of play.

Zak tossed a glance toward his viewing box. Maitlyn was nowhere to be found; only Izabella and her father were holding court. He looked down at the platinum-and-diamond watch on his wrist. He thought she would have been there by then, but she was late. He imagined that she was probably putting the final touches on her formal attire, pairing the perfect shoes with the form-fitting satin-and-lace gown she planned to wear. He looked forward to her making a grand entrance and turning the heads of every man in the room. Imagining that moment lifted his mouth in a slight smile.

Hours later Maitlyn still had not made an appearance. Zak was suddenly concerned, and it showed on his face. He gestured for the cruise director, and the woman tripped over her feet to get to his side.

"Yes, sir, Mr. Sayed. How can I help you, sir?"

"I'm concerned about Ms. Boudreaux. Would you please have someone check my cabin for her?"

The woman nodded. "Not a problem, sir."

Returning his attention to the game, Zak called, pushing in his chips to match Dr. Prentiss's bid. Alexander Lloyd raised, a smug smirk on his face.

Zak lifted his eyes to look at the man. He tried to get a read on what might be in his opponent's hand. Alexander stared back, his eyes wide with excitement.

"You're welcome to fold at any time," Alexander said, shooting glances to the other two players before staring back at Zak.

Zak called again, matching Alexander's raise. Another fifty thousand dollars had been added to the pot. Both Talley and Prentiss folded their hands. The dealer laid out the last card, and Alexander's face flushed a deep red. He struggled to keep a smile on his face. He bid, and once again Zak met the challenge. The dealer called for them to turn out their hands. Alexander took a deep breath before laying a pair of sixes and a pair of aces on the table.

"Two pair," the dealer called.

Zak turned his cards over, not one muscle in his face moving.

"Full house wins," the dealer called, sliding the massive pile of chips in Zak's direction.

Alexander slapped both palms against the table, wearing his frustrations on his sleeves. Zak was not moved by the display.

"This will be the final hand," the dealer declared.

There was a surge of electricity in the room, the crowd's excitement ignited the air. Zak tossed a quick look over his shoulder. There was still no sign of Maitlyn. Something wasn't right, and he could feel it.

With the cards shuffled, the dealer dealt each player two cards facedown. He then laid five cards out on the board: the ace of diamonds, the ace of clubs, the eight of clubs, the six of clubs and the four of clubs. Zak checked his hand and passed the bid on to the next player. Dr. Prentiss went all in, moving ten million dollars into the pot. Ms. Talley stole a quick peek at her hold cards, then pushed all her chips into the pot.

"All in," the dealer chimed. "Nine million."

Alexander played with his chips and then pushed them to the center of the table, as well. "Raise!"

"Raise," the dealer repeated. "Twenty million."

Zak leaned forward, his eyes locked on Alexander. The room was dead quiet, and the silence was almost unnerving. Alexander stared back, confidence painting his expression. Zak studied his stack of chips as he pondered his move, his face revealing little. He looked around the room again, concern for Maitlyn foremost on his mind. Any other time and he would have toyed with Alexander, raising the pot a little at a time. But he wasn't in the mood.

Movement at the door pulled his attention. He watched as the cruise director eased to the captain's side and whispered into the man's ear. His old friend suddenly rushed from the room. At that very moment he was done. His concern for Maitlyn rose with a vengeance. Facing the twenty-million-dollar raise, Zak pushed all his chips in.

"Player is all in," the dealer noted. "Forty million dollars."

Alexander's mouth twisted from one side to the other. He peeked at the two cards in his hand then lifted his eyes back to Zak. "I call," he said. His arrogant tone grated on Zak's last nerve. For the first time since the beginning of the tournament, Zak leaned back in his chair and smiled. Alexander's eyes widened and his face flushed.

"Everyone, turn out please," the dealer called. He nodded at each of them.

Dr. Prentiss turned out a flush, adding a deuce and jack of clubs to make his hand. Ms. Talley nodded. With a pair of fours in the hole, she had a full house. Next, Alexander laid out his cards, smiling brightly. He shot Zak a look, his eyes narrowing slightly.

"Higher full house. Aces over sixes," the dealer announced as he laid out Alexander's hand, adding an ace of hearts and six of spades to the mix.

Zak relaxed, leaning back comfortably in his seat. He slid his hold cards slowly to the center of the table, his eyes still locked with Alexander's. And then he turned them, exposing the five and seven of clubs. The game was won with a straight flush.

"High hand," the dealer announced. "Our tournament winner, Mr. Zakaria Sayed!"

The crowd erupted into thunderous applause and cheers. Enraged, Alexander jumped from the table and stormed out of the room.

Zak stood and buttoned his tuxedo jacket. He shook hands with his fellow players and the dealer. A photographer rushed in to take pictures, but Zak's mind wasn't on having won the tournament. All he wanted was to get Maitlyn.

He headed to the elevators, where he ran into the cruise director, his friend Simon and members of the ship's security team. Stacy looked petrified, and concern pierced Simon's eyes.

"Where is she?" he questioned, looking from one to the other.

Simon took in a deep breath. "We don't know. Someone ransacked your room, and we can't find her anywhere. The entire ship has been searched and I'm having my staff do it all again."

Chapter 15

Pain throbbed through the back of her head as Maitlyn struggled to open her eyes. She was soaking wet and cold, and her body trembled from the chill and fright. Her hands and legs were restrained behind her back, and her mouth had been duct-taped. She was cramped in a small space, with little room to move. Her heart was racing, and it was becoming difficult to breathe.

Maitlyn squeezed her eyes closed tightly as she tried to shake the clouds from her head. She had to be able to think, to figure out where she was and how she was going to get out. The last thing she remembered was dressing for the poker tournament and being excited to go see Zak play. After she had checked her makeup one final time, there had been a knock on the cabin door. Frank and Gerard had stood on the other side, both offering to walk her down to the tournament. She had thanked them for the offer but had declined. As she'd turned to pick up her purse, something sharp had stung her on the back of her neck. She had barely lifted her hand to rub the assaulted spot when she'd felt herself falling forward toward the floor; then everything around her had gone black.

She took another deep breath, desperate to stall the wave of anxiety that was threatening to consume her. She knew that she was moving, a steady *bump, bump, bump* over a hard surface. Maitlyn realized she was in a boat, a speedboat that was cruising at a high speed across the water. Above her she could hear voices but couldn't make out what anyone was saying. She couldn't begin to fathom why the two men had taken her or what they wanted, but knowing she wasn't on the cruise ship frightened her even more.

Maitlyn struggled to make sense of her situation. A speedboat couldn't have been so far out in the ocean. With their next port of call being Greece and the ship scheduled to dock there in the early morning hours, Maitlyn reasoned they had to be headed in that direction, as well. The Greek isles were the closest body of land.

Tears began to drip over her cheeks. If she were on the ship, there was a chance Zak could find her. But she wasn't there, and she wasn't quite sure he'd even know where to begin to look.

"I need to make a call," Zak demanded, moving toward the ship's radio room.

The captain followed on his heels. "We'll be docking in Greece in twenty minutes. I've already radioed ahead and the local police will board once we port."

Zak nodded. "What about the security tapes?"

"I reviewed them personally. Two passengers knocked on your door and entered the cabin shortly before nine. They both exited twenty minutes later. They appear to be speaking with someone in the doorway, but we can't make out who. However, I didn't see her ever exiting the room or anyone else entering."

"I want to speak to those passengers. Who were they?"

Simon gestured toward the security director, who flipped through his notes. "Mr. Frank Barber and Mr. Gerard Bruner," he answered.

Zak bristled. "I need to make that call," he repeated.

Ten minutes later, the ship's operator was connecting him to an unlisted cell phone number. A familiar voice answered on the third ring.

"Hello?"

"We have a problem."

"Where are you?" Kendrick Boudreaux asked.

"Docking in Greece."

"Where's my sister?"

Zak took a deep breath before answering. "They took her." As he disconnected the call, Zak knew there wasn't anything else that needed to be said. He knew beyond any doubts that if Kendrick weren't in Greece before the ship docked that he'd be there shortly after.

As the morning sun rose, the Hellenic Coast Guard was executing a massive search for Maitlyn in the waters of the Mediterranean Sea. With the local police on his heels, Zak entered his stateroom for the first time since leaving it the night before. Both levels were in complete disarray with furniture overturned and papers tossed about. Someone had gone to great lengths to make them think that more had happened there than just Maitlyn disappearing.

As Zak repeated the answers to questions he'd been asked over and over again, he knew that he had far more information than they did. He had no problems playing the role of suspect as the chief of police tried to piece together his own assumptions of what might have happened. Thus far, he seemed convinced that this was a story of a domestic dispute gone awry, a lover's spat that had reached a point of no return, resulting in him hurling her body off the balcony to the ocean below. For the moment, though, Zak knew that wherever Maitlyn was, she was safe. He had something her kidnappers wanted more—two hundred and fifty million dollars.

The local constable was growing frustrated with Zak, as he showed no ounce of emotion. Zak was sure that the officer would have felt better if he had been a sobbing lunatic, but his stoic demeanor made the pop-eyed man nervous. Detective Angelo Rossi finally asked him outright if he'd killed the woman and tossed her body off the side of the ship.

Zak's stare was ice-cold, daggers piercing the room. "No."

The two men stood staring at each other harshly before the detective moved on with his questioning.

The ship's cruise director shook her head vehemently. "Mr. Sayed arrived at the casino early and was there through the end of the tournament. He never left the room."

The cruise line's chief security officer tried to appear commanding. Slight in frame with a voice that sounded like a mouse scratching for attention made that hard for him to do. "We have Ms. Boudreaux on tape talking to another passenger on the upper decks at five-thirty. His name is Lloyd. Alexander Lloyd."

Zak bristled; that information was something he hadn't known.

The security guy continued, "Less than four minutes later, we see her returning to Mr. Sayed's suite. Mr. Sayed exited that same room shortly after seven. We can't find Ms. Boudreaux on tape anymore after that."

The detective nodded. "I want to see all those tapes, please."

Zak paid particular attention to Frank and Gerard as the detective questioned them about their involvement. Both swore that Maitlyn had been well and good when they'd come to the door.

"She said that she was feeling under the weather, motion sickness from the bad weather," Gerard stated. "We offered to walk her down to the casino," he added, "but she said she would come along later."

"I feel horrible," Alexander intoned. "She was such a delightful woman. I wish I knew more, but I was playing cards with her boyfriend all night."

When Zak had heard enough he moved toward the door. Detective Rossi gestured for one of his officers to stop him, and the young lieutenant moved to block his way. He cut an eye at the man, then slowly turned to his commander.

"Rushing off somewhere, Mr. Sayed?" Detective Rossi asked.

"I need to go ashore," Zak said. "I need to contact her family."

"One of my officers will take you to the station."

Zak shook his head. "That won't be necessary. There's a little coffee shop as you exit the dock. You'll be able to find me there."

Rossi's eyes widened. "Mr. Sayed," he started, "while we're investigating this case, it's best you—"

Zak interrupted the man. "Unless you're arresting

me, I'll be at the coffee shop. Then I'll return to the ship. You have my word."

After a moment's hesitation, the man nodded, and Zak rushed pass him.

The espresso shop was full; a host of cruise ship passengers packed in to partake of the baklava and assorted Greek pastries. Zak stepped through the door and took a quick glance around. He moved to an empty table in the corner. When a young waiter came to the table, he ordered a cup of their Greek coffee, a true coffee lover's brew, black as hell, strong as death and sweet as love, according to the shop's motto.

After connecting his laptop to the store's Wi-Fi, he signed into his email. The message was at the top of his inbox list. The sender was unknown, the ID a series of numbers, but the message text was crystal clear. There was a photograph of Maitlyn holding the morning's newspaper and an offshore Panamanian bank account number. He had until the ship left dock that afternoon to transfer his two-hundred-and-fifty-million-dollar winnings into it.

A dark shadow loomed over his computer screen, and he lifted his eyes to find Kendrick Boudreaux staring down at him.

"You lost my sister?"

"I will get her back," Zak offered with regret but assurance.

Kendrick shook his head as he took a seat in the chair opposite of him. "You have a tail!" he said as he gestured for the waiter, tilting his head toward a blond-haired woman sitting in the opposite corner.

Zak nodded. "Local police. The detective thinks I strangled Maitlyn and threw her body overboard."

"You might wish you had when we get her back and she finds out she got caught up in one of our missions. Why did they take her anyway? What happened to our bait?"

Zak hesitated for a moment before responding. "I think they figured out that Maitlyn was my Achilles' heel. The best way to get to me was to threaten to hurt her."

Kendrick eyed him curiously. "Why would they think you and Maitlyn were that close?"

Zak met Kendrick's intense stare, but he had no words.

Kendrick suddenly shook his head. He jumped to his feet, his face skewed in disbelief. "My sister? Oh, *hell* no!" he snapped as he slammed back in his seat. "I should bust you in your head. Didn't anyone ever teach you the rules?" Kendrick counted off on his fingers. "You don't mess with your buddy's sisters. And you don't sleep with your best friend's mother." Kendrick tossed up his hands. "There's some shit you just don't do!"

Zak nodded. "I would never sleep with your mother."

The two men continued to eye each other intently. Zak broke the silence, his voice coming in a loud whisper. "I love Maitlyn, and she loves me."

Kendrick shook his head. "If anything happens to my sister, I will kill you."

Zak smiled. "I know you'll try. But I'm not going to let anything happen to Maitlyn. I promise you that."

Kendrick let out a deep sigh, his head still shaking slowly.

"How'd they get her out of the room and off the ship?" Zak asked.

"That took some skills. The two of them tossed her off your balcony. She was wearing a life vest with a GPS chip. They had a boat waiting nearby to fish her out. I'm thinking they drugged her, because she didn't put up a fight. There's no way my sister would have gone over the side without kicking and screaming if she'd been conscious. That's going to piss her off, too."

"How long was she in the water?"

"Longer than you or I would have liked now that I know it was Maitlyn who'd been tossed overboard," Zak said in an attempt to slightly ease Kendrick's tension.

Zak studied Kendrick from across the table. He knew he had let him down. There wasn't much he didn't know about his partner; the two had been assigned more cases together than either cared to count. Zak's career had started with Interpol, the network of police forces from countries all over the world. Kendrick had been with the FBI. Both had been recruited for a special joint unit of the Secret Service within months of each other. Their partnership had worked from day one, and Zak couldn't imagine having a better partner by his side. He trusted Kendrick with his life and he knew Kendrick felt the same way. But he also knew that if Kendrick were to trust him with his sister, it would give new dimension to their friendship.

This mission had been two years in the making. What had started as a simple financial fraud case had crossed borders from one side of the world to the other. Identifying the players had taken some serious team work. All the players had been carefully selected and put into place: Izabella, the captain, even Lourdes the waitress. No one had been missed. Izabella should have been the hostage mark. He had never considered that his relationship with Maitlyn would derail that entire scheme but they were prepared with a contingency plan.

Tracking down Alexander Lloyd and learning his dirty secrets had been routine. His many crimes included human trafficking, money laundering and fraud, and he was at a point of desperation, his gambling debts extreme. He had bankrupted his father's business and squandered the millions of dollars owned by Lloyd Banks' account holders. Winning that poker game had been his last hope to gain a foothold toward recovery, and Zak had snatched that from him. They had left Alexander with few options and the temptation had been more than he could resist.

A text message chimed on Kendrick's phone, and he read it quickly. He tossed Zak a quick look. "You need to get back to the ship. The lines are in place. They're ready for you to make that transfer. We'll be able to track it all the way into Alexander's back pocket."

"This doesn't feel right to me," Zak said. "Are you sure our agents have an eye on Maitlyn?"

Kendrick nodded. "She's not far from here. But what's *really* bothering you?" he asked.

"This feels personal."

"That will happen when you sleep with my sister and she gets kidnapped," Kendrick said sarcastically.

Zak shook his head. He suddenly shifted forward in his seat. "Alexander knew about Debra. But how did he know? And why would he taunt Maitlyn with it? That's been racking my brain for days now."

Kendrick shifted forward in his own seat, and the

two huddled together. "What did you find?" he questioned.

"That's it. I haven't been able to figure it out. But there's something to Alexander Lloyd that we're missing, and I can't risk Maitlyn being hurt because of it."

Kendrick stood up. "I'll make some calls. You head back to the ship and make the transfer, and then meet me back here. We'll go pick up Maitlyn together."

Zak watched as Kendrick made his way out the door. He dropped a tip onto the table and headed to the opposite corner of the room. The female officer was wide-eyed as she looked up at him. "I'm headed back to the ship," he said. "Please let Detective Rossi know."

Chapter 16

Maitlyn had been fighting a fever since they'd taken her off the boat. Her whole body hurt, and she could feel the tight congestion settling deep in her chest. She'd developed a nasty cough that sounded like she was going to bring up a lung.

She dragged her body off the mattress on the floor, moving to the door. It was locked from the other side, and Maitlyn banged on it for the umpteenth time, hopeful that the harsh rap might draw someone's attention. She knew that she was in a basement; no hint of a window allowed in any light. The space was damp and chilly, and the smell of mildew filled the room.

She'd only seen one person since she'd been dumped there, an elderly woman whose English was as bad as Maitlyn's Greek. The woman had brought her a bowl of soup, a loaf of bread, a pitcher of water, a thin blanket and an empty bucket. Then she'd made Maitlyn sit with a copy of the morning newspaper and snapping her photograph with a digital camera. Someone else had let the woman in and then had let her out. Two sets of footsteps moved back up a flight of stairs.

Maitlyn didn't know if she should be scared or not. She still didn't have a clue what was going on or why she was being held. The old woman didn't have any answers for her. She shook her head, fighting back the tears that threatened to fall from her eyes.

Moving back to the tattered mattress, Maitlyn lay down on her side and pulled the blanket over her shoulders. She drew her knees to her chest, curling her body in fetal position. She wanted Zak. She would have given anything to be in his arms. And she hated thinking that might never happen again.

The money transfer had gone through without incident. Within minutes of delivery, Zak received an email telling him where he could find Maitlyn. He changed from his suit to a pair of black nylon jogging pants, sneakers and a T-shirt. He was headed toward the exit when one of the ship stewards stopped him to deliver an urgent message that the captain needed to see him as soon as possible. Stealing a quick glance at his watch, Zak hustled his way to the helm. Simon was standing at the entrance to the control room. The two men locked gazes.

"You received a message. Your assistant needs you to call. She said it's important."

Zak took a deep breath. "Can you get me a line out?"

The captain nodded. "It'll have to be quick. We need to prepare for departure. We'll pull out in two hours."

"I appreciate it," Zak said as the captain led him to his private office to connect the call.

Minutes later, Bailey Chase, a former technical analyst and communications specialist, picked up the line.

She was a computer wizard with extraordinary technical abilities, and Zak relied heavily on her skill set.

"What did you find out?" Zak asked.

"Debra had a brother."

"Excuse me?" Shock rang in Zak's tone. "Debra was an only child."

"Debra's mother had a son she gave up for adoption. The adoption had been arranged by the Catholic Church, and the records were sealed. The child was adopted by Talon and Pietra Hernandez. The adoptive parents were killed in a car accident when her brother was two years old. He spent a year at a convent children's home in England and was then adopted by Max and Kirsten Lloyd. Alexander Lloyd is Debra's biological brother."

Zak was stunned, taken aback by the news. After a moment of silence, he asked, "Did she know?"

"Probably not. Those records are still sealed. I kind of went through the back door to get them. You know how I do."

"Is it possible Alexander knows?"

"There's a notation in his file that Alexander visited the convent looking for information on his parentage but was denied. Thanks to a very generous donation from one Zakaria Sayed and Debra Mercado, the convent's records were converted to digital data the year before his visit. You and I both know that the right amount of money in the right palm and those files might have easily been left open on a desk or public computer for someone to read. Or someone like me could've just hacked in.

"And something else you should know," Bailey continued. "Last year the agency declassified the files on

Debra's death. If her brother wanted the details, he would have had no problems finding them."

A wave of panic hit Zak in his midsection. He sucked in a swift inhale of air. Not bothering to say goodbye Zak disconnected the call. Something in his gut told him Alexander had no intentions of letting Maitlyn go.

A white panel truck was parked at the corner of the Cephalonia neighborhood when the taxi dropped Zak off in front of the home where he hoped to find Maitlyn. Zakaria stepped out and saw that Kendrick and the backup team were already in place.

Zak adjusted his earphones, finagling the volume. "Hey, can you hear me?"

Kendrick's voice sounded back within seconds. "Loud and clear, brother-in-law."

Zak brushed a lazy hand past his ear, his fingers grazing the earpiece in his ear. He then glanced over the landscape, looking for anything that might be out of the norm. "Anything yet?" he asked.

"Negative," Kendrick stated. "Just head to the door, and, please, watch your back. We don't know what to expect. Besides, I really want to see my sister kick your ass for getting her into this mess."

Zak nodded. *So do I,* he thought. Though, he hadn't shared the information he'd received from Bailey with anyone. He knew it would have made them both anxious, and, because he was already on pins and needles, he needed Kendrick to be calm.

He was worried about Maitlyn, and he couldn't afford to let it show. The anxiety was reminiscent of his experience with Debra. He had been deep undercover for over one year in pursuit of a renowned drug lord.

Debra, wanting to surprise him for his birthday, had shown up unexpectedly. Trying to save his cover, he'd treated her badly. Her reaction had been just enough for the drug cartel to go digging. Researching Debra led them right back to his true identity. Once unmasked, revenge against him was inevitable. He'd come home to find her petite body riddled with bullets. He'd shown the drug lord more mercy, only firing one shot to the man's head. After, he'd handed in his gun and badge, retreating to Morocco. Until Kendrick had come calling, reviving life back into him. Now, here they were, him scared of what Debra's brother had in store for Maitlyn.

Zak took a deep breath to steel his nerves. As he approached the home's front door, a car pulled into the narrow driveway and an attractive woman jumped out excitedly.

"So sorry I'm late!" she exclaimed, rushing to shake Zak's hand. "Mr. Sayed, I'm Phoebe Christos."

Confusion washed over Zak's face.

"The real estate agent," she added.

Zak nodded as the woman continued talking; her exuberance was overwhelming. "You were probably expecting Mr. Kalfas, but he was called away on an emergency. I was very excited to be able to step in and take his place." She suddenly turned and gave him a once-over. "Was your wife not able to join you?" she asked.

Zak shook his head. "I'm hoping she'll be along shortly," he said.

The agent smiled brightly as she used a key to open the front door. "Well, this home is priced at one hundred and fifty-eight thousand euros. It has two bedrooms, one bathroom and five hundred and fifty square meters of outdoor space and a basement. You have fabulous views of the sea and beach and it's close to a number of taverns and cafés. Come see," she said, not bothering to take a breath until she'd actually stopped speaking.

Zak's eyes skated quickly about the space. The home was empty; there was no sign of Maitlyn. He paced from one room to another, trying to make sense of the situation. His anxiety levels were steadily rising.

The real estate agent was still chattering on and on until Zak interrupted her. "Excuse me, but who made this appointment. Do you have a name?"

She looked at him awkwardly. "Well, you did. Didn't you?"

Zak took a deep breath.

"Why don't I show you the upstairs," she said. Zak raced in that direction before the woman could finish the sentence.

The only piece of furniture in the entire home was a small wooden table that sat in the center of the finished master space. A legal-size white envelope addressed to Zakaria sat on top. Zak tore it open, pulling a folded sheet of paper and a picture from inside. He was immediately alarmed by the image of Maitlyn—she clearly wasn't in good health. He felt his heart fracture. The message was short.

An eye for an eye. Your family for mine.

Maitlyn heard his voice, but nothing the man was saying made sense to her. She knew the voice, but she couldn't open her eyes to put a face to it. He was telling her a story about Zak and his sister and something bad that Zak had done. She tried to tell him she didn't know what he was talking about, but the words weren't there.

She could hardly breathe, and each breath she took felt as if it had to pass through thick mud to get to her lungs. Her lips were parched and cracked; her mouth was dry and her stomach was empty. Her body was hot, and all she wanted was a cool breeze to bring her some relief.

The man was angry, screaming harsh words at her, but she didn't have the strength to tell him his problems had nothing at all to do with her. She felt him grab her arm and try to pull her to her feet, but she could not move. Dead weight held her hostage against the floor.

The man was still screaming about family. She tried to smile. She had family, and they loved her like she loved them. Her mind quickly escaped to images of her and Zak starting a new family. Somewhere in the clouds that filled her head footsteps echoed off in the distance, the screaming man's voice fading with the wind. Sensing that she was alone again, Maitlyn blew a soft sigh. Within seconds, she drifted slowly back to sleep, Zak's name a soft whisper against her lips.

Kendrick and a team of agents rushed into the home. "Where is she?"

Zak passed him the photograph and the letter, briefing him on Alexander's connection to his past. "Does anyone have eyes on him?" Zak asked.

"He's back on the *Coastal Galaxy*. It's pulling out of port as we speak."

"I thought you said the intel was good? That we had eyes on her?" Zak asked.

"It was good. They dropped her off here. We haven't taken our eyes off this place since."

"Then where is she?" Zak suddenly shouted. He moved to the window to stare out of it. Across the way an old woman was standing in her front yard. When she caught sight of Zak in the window, she hurried inside her home. He turned to the real estate agent.

"Who owns this house?"

"The bank does."

"Lloyd Banks?"

She nodded. "They own this one and many more in this neighborhood."

"Help me understand," he said. "We're sitting high up in the cliffs here, but you said this house has a basement?"

She nodded. "This property and the others belonged to one family many, many years ago. The basements connect to a series of tunnels that run from one home to the other. A few have been concreted up but one or two are still open."

Zak and Kendrick both made a dash for the downstairs. The basement was damp and dark, and Kendrick tossed his friend a flashlight. "We need to split up. Keep your eyes open," Kendrick said.

One or two tunnels turned out to be an elaborate network of stone-walled underground tunnels. Both men ran into dead end after dead end. Just as Zak's frustration was about to implode, Kendrick's voice chimed in his earpiece.

"I've got her!"

For three days straight Maitlyn slept. The doctors and nurses at IASO General Hospital in Athens were zealous in caring for her. From the moment she was admitted, Zak never left her side. He slept in the chair at her bedside.

"You really need to go get some rest," Kendrick admonished. "I'll keep an eye on her."

Zak shook his head. "When she wakes up, I plan to be right here."

Kendrick paused. "You really do love her—don't you?"

Zak met his friend's stare. Kendrick held up his hand. "You don't need to answer. I haven't seen you look that sappy since...well, you know."

"I almost got her killed, too," Zak whispered.

Kendrick let out a heavy breath. "But you didn't. She's fine. You're fine. I'm fine. Life is good."

"Have you told your family?"

He shook his head. "No, and I hate it, but this will be one secret the three of us will have to take to our graves. When that cruise ship pulls out of the port in London, Maitlyn will be on it. The family and I will be there to welcome you both home."

Zak shook his head.

"I'm not going back. I'm going to fly from here to Morocco and stay there for a few months."

Kendrick leaned forward in his seat and propped his elbows on his thighs. "Why? What about Mattie?"

Zak stood up and walked to the other side of the bed, staring down at her. She looked peaceful, the color back in her cheeks. If she had just been asleep and not in a hospital bed, he would have climbed in by her side, cradling her in his arms. He brushed a slow hand across her cheek. She didn't stir.

Zak moved back to his chair; Kendrick still eyeballed

him. "I put her life in danger, Kendrick. I can't risk that happening again. I can't lose her like I lost Debra. It will be better this way, and you know it."

He watched as Kendrick nodded his head in understanding. Kendrick then stood up and moved to his sister's bedside. "Then you need to leave now before she wakes up. If she wakes up and you're here and then you leave, it will devastate her. Leave now. The mission is finished, and I will fix the rest the best I can."

Chapter 17

Maitlyn was astonished, still unable to grasp the mechanics of everything that had happened to her. Waking up to her brother by her bedside had almost given her a heart attack. But waking to Zak's absence had broken her heart completely. She still had more questions than answers, and for the first time in a long time Kendrick seemed more motivated to respond.

"Does anyone in the family know you work for the Secret Service?" she asked.

"It's a covert division of the Secret Service. An international contingency of multiple agencies."

Maitlyn stared at him, not amused by his correction.

He smiled as he answered her question. "Senior does. He's my emergency contact. And now you."

She shook her head. "I still can't believe any of this," she said throwing up her hands.

Kendrick shrugged. "I hate that this happened to you, Mattie. Zak and I both would have done anything to stop it. But you can't ever tell anyone. And you definitely can't tell Mommy or even Daddy this story. No one can ever know what Zak and I do for a living."

"So he really didn't win the poker tournament?"

"No, he really won. In fact, once we put the hand-cuffs on Alexander Lloyd, they redirected his money right back to him. Zak's gambling skills are why they chose him for this operation."

"And Alexander is really in jail?"

"Interpol took him into custody when the ship docked in Italy. When it's done and finished, he'll do a minimum of thirty years to life. Frank and Gerard, as well. In addition to all the other charges we have against them, they'll also stand trial for your kidnapping."

She nodded. "So, Zak was just pretending. About everything?"

Kendrick wrapped an arm around her shoulders as tears misted in her eyes.

"Zak had a mission to complete, and he did that. And now he's off to his next mission. But he asked me to thank you and to tell you that he hoped your cruise was everything you had wished since that first day."

Maitlyn was speechless, not wanting to believe her brother's words. That Zak wasn't the man she'd come to know.

After their private flight into Heathrow Airport, a limousine had been waiting to take them to the South-ampton port where the *Coastal Galaxy* was docked in wait. She was still not 100 percent healthy; a respira-tory infection and pneumonia had ravaged her immune system. But Kendrick insisted that her cruising back to New Orleans would heal her body, her head and her heart. She wanted desperately to believe him.

Maitlyn had told her brother everything about her time with Zakaria. She'd been convinced that what they shared had been more than just a vacation fling. Nothing could have convinced her that Zak hadn't felt the same way. Kendrick had been sympathetic, insisting that he knew Zak had not intended to purposely deceive her.

"He's really a good guy and a true friend," Kendrick had said. "But he's also great at his job and he'll do whatever he has to."

"So he used me?"

Kendrick shook his head vehemently. "I asked him to look out for you. He has a protective nature. And he liked you. He wanted you to have a great time. To take your mind off the divorce."

She didn't bother to tell her brother that Zak had claimed to love her. And she didn't tell him that she had loved him back.

Kendrick boarded the cruise ship, and the captain stood nearby to welcome her return. Both men walked her back to the luxury suite that she had shared with Zak. Her heart sank. "I'd rather stay in my original room if that won't be a problem," she said.

Simon shook his head. "No problem at all. I'll have the staff move your things," he said.

"Are you sure?" Kendrick questioned. "The agency paid good money for this suite. I'd hate to see it go to waste."

"Mommy and Daddy paid good money for my cabin," she answered, not bothering to add that there were too many memories of her and Zak in that room.

Kendrick shook his head. "Okay."

He walked her down to her cabin and got her comfortably settled inside. Maitlyn crawled into the bed and pulled the covers up over her head.

"Are you going to be okay, Maitlyn?" Kendrick asked in a concerned tone.

She nodded her head but didn't bother to lift it from beneath the blanket.

"Are you sure?" he asked again.

"Go, Kendrick. I'll be fine," she said. "I'll see you in New Orleans."

He leaned down to kiss her cheek. "I love you, kiddo!"

She nodded, nothing else left for her to say.

"I cannot believe that you had all that time alone and didn't get laid. That makes no sense to me," Tarah said, helping Maitlyn unpack her luggage.

Maitlyn shook her head, showing her annoyance. "I didn't go on my cruise to get laid. I went to relax and revive myself."

"I would have gotten laid, too," Tarah stated. "At least once. Didn't you even try to get with Kendrick's friend? That man was so *foine!*"

For a quick moment, Maitlyn felt as if a knife had been stuck straight through her heart. The pain felt unbearable, and it took every ounce of energy she had not to burst into tears. She missed Zak. She missed him so much that every time she thought about him, hurt consumed her. She still couldn't comprehend that what had happened between them was just him performing his job. She had trusted him and felt safe with him. He had told her he loved her, and she had believed him with every fiber of her being. It suddenly felt as if someone had reached into her chest and snatched the life from her. She doubled over in a fit of coughing, fighting to catch her breath.

Her mother rushed in from the doorway, patting her heavily on the back. "You okay, baby. Tarah, get your sister some water, please."

Tarah rushed into the bathroom and grabbed a paper cup, then filled it from the faucet. She hurried back, passing the cup to her.

Maitlyn took a sip. She took deep breaths, clearing her throat. There were tears in her eyes.

Her mother eyed her warily. "I hate that you went on that cruise and caught a cold. Probably was that change in weather from country to country."

Maitlyn nodded. "I guess," she finally said.

"What's this?" Tarah said, pulling a white paper bag from the inside of her luggage. She then pulled a photograph from the inner lining.

"Oh, my!" Tarah exclaimed, turning the image for her mother to see.

Maitlyn inhaled swiftly. She'd completely forgotten about that arrival photo, her standing in Zak's arms. Seeing it made her want to cry all over again.

"Isn't that special," Katherine crooned. "Y'all look quite nice together."

Maitlyn shook her head. "They took it by accident. They thought we were a couple."

"Well, you'd make an attractive couple. I really liked that young man. Did I tell you that your daddy and I met him when we went to visit Kendrick last year?"

"No, you didn't," Maitlyn said softly.

Her mother nodded. "I probably told Kamaya."

"You told me, too, Mommy," Tarah chimed.

"Yes, I did. He was a nice young man and not married, if I remember."

Tarah jumped onto the bed beside her, her legs

crossed Indian-style. "Are you sure something didn't go on with you and Mr. Sayed?" she said, bumping her shoulder against Maitlyn's. Her grin was a mile wide as she eyed Maitlyn suspiciously.

"So, what's been going on since I left?" Maitlyn asked, changing the subject.

For the next hour Maitlyn listened as her mother and sister caught her up on all the family gossip. She was excited to learn that her brother Guy and his wife, Dahlia, had learned that the baby they were expecting was actually twins.

"Oh, how sweet!" she said. "Dahlia must be so excited."

Tarah nodded. "She is. You know they'd already picked out names. It was going to be Sidney if it's a boy, after Sidney Poitier, and Cicely if it's a girl, after Cicely Tyson. She says she has to pick out two more now, just in case she doesn't get a boy-girl combo. Personally, I like Halle and Idris if they plan to stick to the movie star theme."

"I don't know how Guy is going to do that new television show and help with the babies," her mother mused.

"It won't be a problem. He'll be done shooting by the time the babies are here, and then he'll have six months before he has to be back for the new season," Maitlyn offered.

"I still think Dahlia is going to need some help. I may go to Los Angeles and stay with them for a while," Katherine said, falling into a moment of reflection.

Or I might, Maitlyn thought. Anything to get her mind off having two failed relationships under her belt.

It had been almost two months since Maitlyn had been home, and life felt brighter with each new day.

Throwing herself into her work had kept her from thinking about Zak and their late summer affair. She'd finally gotten to a point where hearing his name didn't make her want to burst into tears. Now there were moments when thinking about him brought her the sweetest pleasure. The experience had taught her much about herself, and she realized that she was even stronger than she'd realized. Despite the loss, her spirit was still intact.

For weeks she'd been helping her brother Darryl and his fiancée, Camryn Charles, plan their wedding. They were tying the knot on New Year's Eve with a simple ceremony and spectacular fireworks reception. The guest list included six hundred friends, family and business associates. With their busy schedules, pinning the duo down to make decisions had become quite the challenge.

With the bride and bridesmaids dress fittings scheduled for that morning, Maitlyn knew she had to get up and get dressed. She had a long list of phone calls and confirmations to make, and intuition told her the day was going to be busier than she preferred. As she thought about all she had to do, she became exhausted.

The following day she was scheduled to fly to Los Angeles to visit her brother Guy and meet her new niece and nephew. The twins had come a few weeks early and all the family was taking turns giving the new parents a hand. Guy was on tap for a new movie role and Maitlyn was on track to negotiate him a contract that would afford him the most time with his new family. She also needed to research distributors for her sister Kamaya's new business. Maitlyn had her hands full, and she liked it that way. As long as she kept busy, she didn't have the time or the energy to think about what she might be missing with Zakaria Sayed. There was no place for Zak to fill all her waking thoughts. Every day she could keep it that way was a good day.

She threw her legs off the side of her bed and sat upright. Her eyes shifted to the framed photograph on her nightstand, the image of her and Zak arriving on their cruise. That first month she'd kept it hidden away in a drawer, hating to even think about it. But now she'd set it on her nightstand and left it there. When she looked at it, she was reminded that she'd had a wonderful time and, for a few weeks, she'd felt very much loved.

Chapter 18

"What is wrong with you, Zakaria?" His mother threw him a concerned stare. "You haven't been yourself for months now."

"I'm fine, *Ommah*." Zak picked the last of the ripe lemons from the fruit trees in his mother's courtyard.

His father gave him a sidelong glance as Zack moved about slowly and finally dropped the bowl of fruit onto the table as he took a seat beside the older man. "Have you heard from her?" his father asked.

Zak lifted his eyes to meet his father's stare. He shook his head. "No, *Baba*. And it's for the best."

His father nodded. His mother sucked her teeth as she fanned a dismissive hand. "*Tch!* You are wrong, son."

Both men turned to stare in her direction.

"This is not best for you. You are hiding away in that house of yours. We barely see you, and when we do, you are a mere semblance of yourself. Your joy is gone. There is nothing *best* about that!"

His mother rose from her seat and moved to his side. She reached down to hug his neck and kiss his cheek.

"This is not best for you," she said. Her head shaking, she waved a hand and rushed from the room, attempting to hide her tears.

When the door to her room was closed, his father refilled both their cups with mint tea. "You really need to speak with her."

Zak shook his head.

His father pursed his lips. "I imagine her heart is just as heavy. You treat her commonly, then turn your back on her."

Zakaria bristled. "I didn't, *Baba.*"

"But you did. You made her believe that you loved her. She trusted that, and she gave herself to you. Then what did you do? You abandoned her like she was nothing."

Tears pierced Zak's eyes. His body tensed defensively as he leaned forward in his seat. "I had to protect her, *Baba.*"

His father shrugged. "If you love her, you protect her by being by her side. You protect her by ensuring she wants for nothing. You give her sons and daughters to love. You commit all of yourself to her, and you let her be your partner. You cannot turn your back on her and say you are protecting her. There is no love in that."

Zak shook his head. "It's been too long. She is probably happy now."

His father laughed. "She loved you with everything in her soul. I'm certain she is as miserable as you are."

Kendrick laughed into the receiver, the chortle core deep.

"Why is that funny?" Zak asked.

"Because the two of you are just alike."

"Does she think about me?"

His friend laughed again. "She does, but she doesn't say it. I see it on her face, that is, when she sits still long enough."

"So what do I do?" Zak asked.

"I'm not the one to ask, Zak. I realize I didn't give either one of you any good advice. You're on your own with this one, my friend."

As Zak disconnected the call, his mother moving behind him made him jump. "*Ommah,* I didn't see you there," he said.

"I figured as much," she answered, having overheard the conversation. She pointed to his cell phone, her eyebrows raised.

Zak lifted the device. "Oh. I was talking with Kendrick Boudreaux."

His mother nodded. "About his sister?"

Zak met her gaze. He didn't bother to answer.

"Did it help?" he mother asked.

"No," Zak finally answered. "He didn't know how to help me."

His mother smiled. "You men!" she said, her smile bright.

He smiled with her, shrugging his shoulders. His mother headed back toward the door and then suddenly stopped, spinning back around on her heels. She stared at him for a brief moment before speaking. "If you love her, Zakaria, tell her. If you must, beg her forgiveness. But to do that, son, you must go to her." She moved to his side and kissed his cheek as she continued. "When a woman loves a man she wants him to be just that. A man! Take charge. Tell her what will be. If Maitlyn loves you like I think she did, she will happily follow your lead."

Zak chuckled softly. "You say that like it will be so easy."

His mother laughed with him. "When love is right, it usually is."

Maitlyn flipped through papers scattered across the kitchen table. She turned briefly to stare out the window. She swiped a hand across her eyes and took a deep breath before turning her attention back to the work before her.

"Hey, you," Kendrick said as he moved back into the room.

Looking up, Maitlyn smiled. "Hey, yourself. I see you made it home safe and sound."

Kendrick nodded. "It was a good vacation," he said, meeting her gaze.

"Did you meet any old friends?" she asked.

Her brother smiled as he nodded his head. "One of them asked about you. I told him you were doing really well."

Maitlyn smiled and nodded. They'd become closer since he'd shared his secrets with her. She also worried more when he disappeared for weeks at a time. Seeing him eased that worry. Hearing that Zakaria was also doing well made her feel better, too.

"So, what are you up to?" Kendrick asked.

"Just making sure everything is covered for the reception tomorrow. I need to make sure the fire chief has a copy of the permit for the fireworks."

"You work too hard, sis," he said. "You'll need your own vacation once this party is over."

Maitlyn rolled her eyes. "Uh, no, thank you. I think I'm done with vacations for a very long while."

Kendrick nodded. "I need to say something to you," he started, dropping down against the cushioned seat across from her. "I gave that mutual friend of ours some bad advice. I thought we were protecting you. With everything we're involved in, it just felt safer. But now I realize I was wrong."

Before Maitlyn could respond, their mother entered the room. Katherine tossed them both a look and smiled brightly. "I don't mean to interrupt you two. I'm glad you have each other to talk to."

"It's no problem, Mom," Kendrick said, standing back up. "We're done. Maitlyn needs to get back to work." He leaned and kissed her, and then moved around the center island to hug and kiss his mother.

When he was gone, Katherine moved to the table where she sat. She and Maitlyn locked gazes.

"Is everything okay, Mommy?" Maitlyn asked, unnerved by the look her mother was giving her.

"I told you once that there was nothing any of my kids could do that I wouldn't find out about. Remember?"

Maitlyn nodded. "Yes, ma'am."

"Your daddy and I don't keep any secrets. Not even the ones you kids think we do. If your daddy knows it, I know it and vice versa. And I agree with your brother. I think he was very wrong. How can he give you advice on love and relationships when he's too scared to have one of his own? Zakaria is a good man. If he wasn't, he wouldn't be Kendrick's friend and you wouldn't be in love with him."

Maitlyn's eyes widened, a tear rolling across her cheek.

Her mother laughed. "Your old mama doesn't miss a trick. I keep telling you kids that!"

Boudreaux Towers stood majestically in the downtown area. The multilevel office complex was a work of art in the New Orleans business district, unlike anything ever seen before. The brainchild of Mason Boudreaux, Maitlyn's oldest brother, the building had just been completed under the direction of their brother Darryl and his new wife. Glowing with light to celebrate the holiday season, the building was spectacular.

Maitlyn had taken the entire penthouse floor, with its magnificent views of the city, and had transformed it to a winter wonderland for the newly married Darryl and Camryn Boudreaux. She stood by the windows, taking in the magnitude of it all. They were only an hour from welcoming in the New Year, and she felt a sense of accomplishment wash over her. But something was still missing.

On the dance floor, the bride and groom were grinning as they danced with family and friends. All her brothers and sisters and her parents were on the floor, gyrating to the beat of the music. The entire Stallion family, Mason's wife, Phaedra, her brothers, Matthew, Mark, Luke and John Stallion were on the dance floor, as well, along with their wives, having a great time. Their conjoined families were happy, and their joy made Maitlyn smile.

It could have been perfect, Maitlyn thought, if only... She shook the thought from her mind. She was suddenly distracted when Kendrick broke from the group and headed in the direction of the door. Surprise and excitement painted his expression. She turned to look where he stared.

Zakaria Sayed stood in the entrance of the large room. His presence was commanding, and everyone in the room turned to ogle. He first shook hands with Kendrick and then followed the gesture of Kendrick's head that led to Maitlyn.

For a brief moment the two stood staring at each other.

Zak felt emotion swell full and thick in his chest. She was beautiful, and the sight of her was a soothing balm to his heart. She looked exquisite in her gown—the sheer red garment complemented the glow in her complexion. He knew in that moment that he would do anything for her to take him back. Willing his legs to move, he headed in her direction.

As he closed the gap between them, he felt his breath catch deep in his chest. He could feel the fissure in his heart begin to close. He then saw the tears in Maitlyn's eyes; she had moved to meet him halfway. After kicking off her high heels, she threw herself into his arms and wrapped her arms around his neck, hugging him with undeniable passion.

"I'm sorry," Zak said, his breath warm as he whispered into her ear. "Can you forgive me?"

"Don't you ever do that to me again," Maitlyn whispered back.

Zak nodded his head. "I promise."

"I've missed you," Maitlyn murmured.

"I love you, Maitlyn. I've never stopped loving you."

Maitlyn tightened her hold. She began to weep. "I

love you, too," she whispered loudly, wanting to shout it from the rooftop.

Zak pulled back slightly, then plunged his mouth against hers, kissing her deeply. He could feel his soul sliding home and swore he would never leave her again. Outside, fireworks shimmered against the midnight sky. Across the dance floor, hugs and kisses rained around the room as the midnight hour welcomed the New Year and new beginnings.

* * * * *

REQUEST YOUR FREE BOOKS!

2 FREE NOVELS PLUS 2 FREE GIFTS!

KIMANI™ ROMANCE

Love's ultimate destination!

YES! Please send me 2 FREE Harlequin® Kimani™ Romance novels and my 2 FREE gifts (gifts are worth about $10). After receiving them, if I don't wish to receive any more books, I can return the shipping statement marked "cancel." If I don't cancel, I will receive 4 brand-new novels every month and be billed just $5.19 per book in the U.S. or $5.74 per book in Canada. That's a savings of at least 20% off the cover price. It's quite a bargain! Shipping and handling is just 50¢ per book in the U.S. and 75¢ per book in Canada.* I understand that accepting the 2 free books and gifts places me under no obligation to buy anything. I can always return a shipment and cancel at any time. Even if I never buy another book, the two free books and gifts are mine to keep forever.

168/368 XDN F4XC

Name	(PLEASE PRINT)

Address		Apt. #

City	State/Prov.	Zip/Postal Code

Signature (if under 18, a parent or guardian must sign)

Mail to the **Harlequin® Reader Service:**
IN U.S.A.: P.O. Box 1867, Buffalo, NY 14240-1867
IN CANADA: P.O. Box 609, Fort Erie, Ontario L2A 5X3

Want to try two free books from another line?
Call 1-800-873-8635 or visit www.ReaderService.com.

* Terms and prices subject to change without notice. Prices do not include applicable taxes. Sales tax applicable in N.Y. Canadian residents will be charged applicable taxes. Offer not valid in Quebec. This offer is limited to one order per household. Not valid for current subscribers to Harlequin® Kimani™ Romance books. All orders subject to credit approval. Credit or debit balances in a customer's account(s) may be offset by any other outstanding balance owed by or to the customer. Please allow 4 to 6 weeks for delivery. Offer available while quantities last.

Your Privacy—The Harlequin® Reader Service is committed to protecting your privacy. Our Privacy Policy is available online at www.ReaderService.com or upon request from the Harlequin Reader Service.

We make a portion of our mailing list available to reputable third parties that offer products we believe may interest you. If you prefer that we not exchange your name with third parties, or if you wish to clarify or modify your communication preferences, please visit us at www.ReaderService.com/consumerchoice or write to us at Harlequin Reader Service Preference Service, P.O. Box 9062, Buffalo, NY 14269. Include your complete name and address.

KROM13R

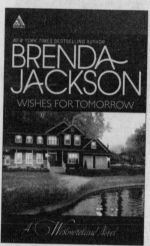